# About the Author

Kimberly Hoff is a mom, wife, and former teacher turned writer. She is a fellow book lover and advocate for reading, and *Secret Moments* is her first published novel. She grew up in Katy, Texas, just outside of Houston, and attended Texas A&M University. She now resides in Buda, Texas, with her husband and two daughters.

# Secret Moments

# Kimberly Hoff

# Secret Moments

Vanguard Press

A CIP catalogue record for this title is available from the British Library.

ISBN 978-1-83794-297-8

This is a work of fiction. Names, characters, businesses, places, events and
incidents are either the products of the author's imagination or used in a
fictitious manner. Any resemblance to actual persons, living or dead, or actual
events is purely coincidental.

*Vanguard Press is an imprint of*
*Pegasus Elliot Mackenzie Publishers Ltd.*
www.pegasuspublishers.com

First Published in 2024

**Vanguard Press**
**Sheraton House Castle Park**
**Cambridge England**

Printed & Bound in Great Britain

# Dedication

To my husband, Stephen – the love of my life.

# Acknowledgments

Since I can remember, I have loved creating stories. Bringing this book to life has been a dream come true for me, and it would not have been possible without my husband, Stephen. With his never-ending support and encouragement, I was able to pursue my love for writing and creating stories. Thank you, babe, for always believing in me and pushing me to follow my dreams. A huge thank you as well to everyone at Pegasus who believed in this story and enjoyed it as much as I enjoyed writing it. To my publishing coordinator and editors. To everyone who has been a part of the process of turning this story into my first ever published book. I am forever grateful. To everyone else who has celebrated and supported me throughout this journey, thank you, thank you, thank you! And finally, to my fellow book lovers, especially romance lovers, thank you for reading my book and for being a part of this exciting journey with me.

# CHAPTER 1

Six months. Six months is all I have left until I will be a college graduate and will be able to get out of this hell hole once and for all. And when I say hell hole, no, I don't mean a dorm room or an apartment I'm sharing with roommates I can't stand. No, when I say hell hole, I mean my home. My *actual* home. The home I have lived in since I was three.

When I turned three, my mother was turning eighteen and was being kicked out of her parents' home. Yes, you did the math correctly. My mother was only fifteen when she had me. It's been just me and her since we moved into this house when I was three years old.

You may be thinking to yourself, Oh wow, only fifteen years apart? I bet you're so close. False. We are not close and never have been. There is no Lorelai and Rory Gilmore mother-daughter relationship in this household.

No, in this house, there is a Loraine and Emma Johnson mother-daughter relationship. One that has only ever been about resentment, alcohol, and belittlement. Oh, and men. A *lot* of men. Gross, creepy ones at that.

My mother blames me for every bad thing that has ever happened in her life. She blames me for not having found the right man yet. "Who would want to marry a woman with an annoying daughter running around the house?" is a comment I have heard many times throughout the years. She blames me for her not being a lawyer, something she apparently has wanted to do since she was a little girl. Instead, because of me, she had to wait tables. That was until my grandparents died when I was ten and she got all the money they had left behind.

Don't get it twisted, we are not wealthy by any means. She got just enough money that allowed her to be able to quit her waitressing job and still let us be able to pay rent, but that's about it. None of that money went toward me, any organizations I wanted to be a part of growing up, or my college career.

Which is why I am twenty-one years old, living at home, and working almost full-time at a coffee shop called Snaps Coffee Joint to be able to pay for it. Which is why it's almost ten p.m. and I'm just now home from my shift, staring at a filthy ass kitchen that I will have to clean before I can head to my room and spend the next few hours studying for an exam I have tomorrow. All while my mother, Loraine, is passed out drunk in her room, and the random truck that is parked in front of our house tells me she is not alone.

This is how it has been for as long as I can remember. Me on my own, taking care of the house, and being responsible for myself. I have had a job since the moment I turned fifteen. My mother used any extra money we had, which was not a lot, on herself and herself only. Making sure she always had her hair and nails done and enough alcohol in the house to help her sleep at night.

Sometimes, I wonder where I would be right now if

my mother had just given me up for adoption. Sometimes, I wish she had. Maybe I would have loving parents who cared for me and supported me. Maybe I would have siblings that were my best friends. Maybe I would have a home that I feel happy in. Maybe. But then I hear about all the kids in foster care and bad homes, and I can at least be thankful that I have never been physically abused and have always had a warm bed to sleep in at night. Even if, on some of those nights, I had to lock my bedroom door because my mother was too drunk to realize how creepy the guys she brought home from the bar were.

Alcohol isn't my mother's only kryptonite. There are also the men. Like I said, there have been a lot of them. She is almost always seeing someone, and if she isn't, she is bringing random guys home from the bar. It isn't hard for her. All she has to do is smile at a man and they go weak in the knees. She knows exactly what to do and what to say to make any guy become wrapped around her finger. Even now, at the age of thirty-six, it is the same as it has always been. She is as beautiful now as she was at eighteen, maybe even more so, and she spends all the leftover money she has left after paying the bills to make sure she stays that way.

My mother is taller than me, about 5'9", with beautiful long blonde hair, blue eyes, tan skin, fake, of course, and a very thin frame. She doesn't even have to work for it either. If she is not out pampering herself or at a bar, she is passed out drunk, so it's quite astonishing really that her physique has stayed the way it has. I guess it's because her diet consists mostly of wine and vodka. I, on the other hand, am shorter, 5'4", with long, thick, brown hair, dark brown eyes, and a curvier frame. I'm a C cup, and I have a good amount of junk in the trunk, something I love about myself. Surprisingly, I love my body. Despite all the comments my mother has made about my weight over the years, I love being short and having curves, and men love it too. Maybe just as much as they love Loraine.

I have never had this desire to be wanted by them like my mother for some reason has. She relies on them and their praise, just as much as she relies on alcohol. She is addicted to both. She feeds off of them and if she goes without one for too long, she becomes bitter and angrier than usual.

Since my mother and I don't share a lot of physical qualities, or mental ones for that matter, I have always wondered about my dad. She does not and will not talk about him, and I have never once in my life seen a picture of him. The only thing she has ever said about him was that he was a cheating jock and that after she told him she was pregnant, he broke up with her within a minute. "This will ruin my football career," he told her.

I have no idea if he ended up having a football career. I know not to dig and ask questions because it only makes my mother angry at me for her not being able to have the life she always wanted. As if it is my fault she slept with her boyfriend at fifteen years old.

So, I hope now you can understand why I am so anxious for these six months to be over and done. In December, I'll graduate from my university with a degree in communications. I chose to major in communications because I felt like it would give me a lot of job opportunities after I graduated. I'm not looking for my dream job here; I'm just looking to get the hell out, and because of my hustle these last few years along with the summer classes I have taken each summer break, I'll be graduating a semester early. Putting this life, this house, and this so-called "mother" behind me for good is just within reach. So close, I can almost taste it.

# CHAPTER 2

I spend an hour cleaning up the mess my mother made today in the kitchen, and then I head to my bathroom to shower off the coffee smell that is still lingering in my hair. I love coffee, and it's the one thing that has gotten me through these last three and a half years of all-nighter study sessions, weeks of summer school, and double shifts at Snaps. It's why I got a job at Snaps in the first place. I had been studying there so regularly that they knew me by name, and when a job opened up and I asked for an application, they hired me on the spot.

I head to my room once my hair is smelling more like vanilla lavender and less like a vanilla blonde roast. I grab my laptop and notes and hunker down for a long night ahead of studying. I usually like to study on campus when I have a big test in the morning, but after a long shift at Snaps, I know I need at least a couple of hours of shuteye in my bed to be able to function the next day. Before I know it, it's five in the morning, and I wake up to my head slamming down onto my textbook. I crawl into bed and let sleep take over.

My alarm blares in my ear after what feels like only five minutes and my head throbs from the lack of sleep. I roll over in my bed and groan. I feel as if I have been out partying all night, not stuck in my room studying for hours.

The worst part is, this is my last summer in college. I should be living it up. I'm supposed to be at pool parties all day, followed by frat parties all night, like every other college student. But since I'm determined to graduate in December, I have to do two courses this summer so that I will have all my credits. And besides, you need to have friends to go to those things. Without the time to join any college groups or organizations, friends aren't something that I've accumulated over the years. My one and only friend is my coworker Jessica.

"Ughhhh!" I groan again as I turn my seven-thirty a.m. alarm off. I've always been a night owl, so mornings are difficult for me. I am by no means a morning person by nature, and the five a.m. bedtimes I've been doing recently have made it even harder to get up.

Heading to my bathroom to shower, in hopes of waking myself up a bit, I can see my mother and her new man-friend saying goodbye at the front door. He is whispering in her ear, and she is giggling like she is sixteen, not thirty-six. I shake my head and roll my eyes when I notice what the man is wearing; an oversized flannel, cargo shorts, shaggy hair, and a shaggy beard to pair with it. And best of all, he has flip flops on his feet. *Flip flops.* I didn't even think you could get into a bar in flip flops. I am not sure why my mother goes for men like this. They are always grungy, have no fashion, and seem so immature. Maybe they make her feel younger or they say exactly what she wants to hear, but my mother is gorgeous, on the outside at least, so I don't understand why the men she sees aren't just as attractive as she is.

"At least I got some last night," she snarls at me.

I hadn't even realized he had left until my mother spoke, breaking me from my thoughts. I was probably making a face, expressing my obvious judgment and distaste. Oh well.

"Oh yah, real jealous, Mom." Rolling my eyes for the second time in under two minutes, I head to the bathroom and slam the door.

Despite what my mother says about me, I know that I, in fact, *do* grab the attention of lots of men. I don't go out much. Well, never really. But I have been hit on and asked out countless times at work and even at school. So, I've been on my fair share of dates when time allows, and if I get an ache that needs to be satisfied, I get it taken care of. Either by men or myself. But I have higher standards than my mother. I don't give my body to just anyone because I know my worth. I do not need a man to make me feel good about myself.

Even though I took a shower just last night, I take extra time in the shower this morning to try and wake my body up after only getting two hours of sleep. I lather up my body and spend extra time grooming, and now that I'm in here, touching every inch of myself, I realize that it has been a while since I've taken care of that sweet spot between my thighs. My fingers linger over my skin and I think about touching myself for a second, especially when a throb starts to form. I've been so busy lately that I can't remember the last time I've felt that release. But I've been in here for too long already, and my test is at nine-thirty and I can't afford to miss it.

Groaning, I turn the shower knob to the left to make the water run ice cold and cringe as I force my body underneath it. I need to clear my head and wake my body up. The cold water stings on my skin, doing exactly that. I can take care of that need later; the only thing I need to do right now is worry about my test.

Quickly, I dry my hair, throw it in a bun, get dressed, grab my school bag, and head for the door. My mother is sitting on the couch in her silk robe she spent too much money on. Money that she has to be running out of by now. She doesn't work or do anything to bring in any sort of income, and with how much she spends on a regular basis, the money my grandparents left has to be running out. She has a cup of black coffee in her hand and is watching her favorite morning show.

"I have class until three and then work until nine." I don't know why I tell her this, because I know she doesn't care, but a part of me likes to pretend we have somewhat of a normal relationship, so anytime I am heading out the door and she is in here, I tell her where I'm going and when I should be getting home. Despite the fact that she has never once asked or cared.

Well, I have a date tonight, and if it goes as I hope, we'll be in the bedroom when you get home, so keep it down, please." She says this as if I have ever been loud or rowdy in this house. I have never even had a friend over.

"Another date? With the lumberjack?" I ask sarcastically.

"Oh, Emma I know no guy wants to have anything to do with you, but the look of jealousy does you no favors," she snarks.

Without responding, I roll my eyes. Again. Is that three times in one morning? A new record. I walk out the door, slamming it behind me. This is how literally every interaction with Loraine is; snarky comments, rolled eyes, and slammed doors. The most frustrating part about that is that she knows that is not true. She has seen me go out on dates or come home in the morning wearing the same clothes I had on the night before. Something about tearing me down makes her feel better about herself, and although I am pretty much used to it at this point, the sting still burns on occasion. She may be awful, but she is still my mother. That desire to be loved by her is not easy to turn off.

"Six months," I tell myself through gritted teeth as I hop in my twenty-year-old maroon Honda Civic with chipped paint and stained seats. It's all I could afford, and I worked my tail off the summer before my junior year of high school at our local grocery store to get her. She may look like a mess, but she has been my escape for the last five years, and I love her to death.

Heading to my test, I am more motivated than ever to pass this course and get my last semester of college on a roll so I can snag myself a decent job and get the hell out of this place and away from my mother once and for all.

# CHAPTER 3

"How was your test?" Jessica asks me as she froths some milk for a latte.

"It was good! I was up 'til five a.m. studying for it, so I felt pretty confident going in," I respond as I pop a blueberry muffin in the toaster oven.

Jessica and I have worked at Snaps Coffee Joint together for almost three years and she is probably my closest friend. Actually, she is my *only* friend. Even though we don't really hang out much outside of work, with how many hours we spend together here during the week, we have gotten to know each other very well. She knows more about my life, including my relationship with my mother, than anyone else. She is a lot like me in the sense that she has worked all through college and is also eager to finish up school, but not for the same reasons. She is extremely adventurous and wants to travel the world after she graduates. She wants to be a photographer, but her parents told her she needed to at least go to college first so she has something to fall back on, but she's been taking pictures on top of working at Snaps and going to school since I have known her. We may not have the same post-college plans, but we really do have a lot in common. Well except for the fact that she is taller and leaner like Loraine, and with deep red hair that is so stunning it stops everyone, both men and women, in their tracks. She is the closest thing I have ever had to a best friend and, even though I'm not sure that I'm her best friend, I am still so thankful just to have her in my life. Our friendship has gotten me through a lot of dark times over the past three years.

"Any new drama with good ole Loraine?" she asks. Since I've shared so many stories about my mother with her, I think she dislikes her just as much as I do, and she has never even officially met her. I love her for that.

"Not really, just the same old. I've been so busy here and with my summer courses that we really haven't been around each other all that much."

"That sounds like a good thing," she encourages.

"Oh, it definitely is! That is my plan until December, and then I am out of that house for good," I say.

"Ugh, I'm so excited for you to get a real job and start your life away from your mom, but I'm going to miss you so much here," she whines, making a cute pouty face.

Jessica isn't graduating until next May, so she will continue working at Snaps through next semester. I don't know whether or not I am going to stay in Houston after I graduate, but I know for sure that if I do, I will be getting all of my coffee here so that I can still see Jessica on a regular basis. On top of getting to see her, they really do have the best coffee in all of town, in my opinion.

"I know, but I promise I'll visit, and we'll have time to hang out somewhere other than work!" I reassure her.

"That's true!" she replies excitedly.

"Oh, you should have seen the guy Loraine slept with last night. So grunge, I just don't get it. I swear her type is a recently divorced forty-year-old man going through a midlife crisis who doesn't know how to dress." I laugh as I give her the gross details of my mother's love life. Our favorite topic of discussion.

"Oh god. I don't get it. I mean, I know your mom is a class A bitch, but she is still a MILF. Like she is so hot, she could get any guy she wants," Jessica responds. She has only seen Loraine through pictures on my mother's social media and some from my phone that I've shown her, but even in pictures, Lorraine is undeniably stunning.

"I know it really is so weird. I think because she's more attractive than them, they give her some sort of validation that she feeds off of."

"Y'all could not be more different," she tells me.

"Trust me, I know." This is a fact I am extremely grateful for; I cannot wait for the day I get to be a mother and be the mom I wish I'd had growing up.

The only good thing Loraine did as a mother was show me what a mom *isn't*. That and I guess she did keep me alive as a child. But she only really did that until I was about ten years old. After that, I was completely on my own. This is why I only refer to her as Loraine or "my mother." She has never been a real mom. I had to learn to make my own meals or order pizza because she would usually pass out drunk by dinner time. We did not do any mother-daughter activities together, like go shopping or get our nails done. Well, Loraine would do these things all the time, she just wouldn't take me with her because she could only afford it for one of us. All my clothes were from resale shops so that way she could save more money for her own wardrobe. They were almost always too big or too small because she didn't know my size and didn't bother to bring me with her so I could at least pick the clothes out myself.

Since I can remember, I have been a loner. I had to be to get through my childhood, and that seeped into my time at school too. I didn't want to rely on anyone but myself. This, along with the fact that I had clothes that did not match nor fit, made it extremely challenging to make friends. I was alone at school and I was alone at home because my mother's need for the attention of men has been going on for as long as I can remember. It didn't get any easier once I got to middle school and high school. She didn't encourage me to join any organizations or sports at school. In fact, it was the opposite. "Why should you get to do all these things when I had to give up my life for you?" she would say to me on a regular basis. Always making sure I never forgot the sacrifices she made to have me.

Except, there were no sacrifices. From what I can remember, me being alive really did not affect her at all, especially once I started school. I took the bus to and from school as soon as I started kindergarten. I would not bother her in the evenings or ask her to take me anywhere. I cooked my own dinners after school and all of my meals on the weekends. And as soon as I turned fifteen, I started working. My first job was stocking shelves and supplies at a gas station down the street from us, so I didn't need a vehicle. I worked there all of sophomore year, and then when junior year started, I got a job at our local grocery store bagging groceries. That is when I saved up enough money to buy a car that was being sold on the side of the road for two thousand bucks. By the grace of God, she is still kicking after all of these years. I do give her lots of love and a pep talk every morning to help keep her going.

Once I had my car, I was able to move up a bit and get a job at Walmart where I made a little more money. I worked there until the summer after my freshman year of college. That's when I got my job at the coffee shop because I knew the hours would work better around my school schedule. Since I didn't really have any friends growing up and I wasn't in any extracurricular activities, I put all of my time that wasn't being taken up by working into studying. This landed me a small academic scholarship, but it only covered about half of my tuition. I make just enough money to pay for college and eat cheap meals, and I am still buying my clothes from second-hand shops, but at least they fit.

So, there you have it. I've been on my own for as long as I can remember. My mother has never been a mom. I would categorize her more as a terrible roommate. There have been no sacrifices made on her end, even though she seems to think so and will hold that lie over my head every chance she gets. Even the bed I sleep in she bought with my grandma and grandpa's money, and I am sure that it was the cheapest one she could find.

Loraine has taught me one thing and one thing only, and that is how NOT to be a loving parent. I dream at night about being a mom and having children. I imagine reading them a book every night before bed, going to their soccer games or recitals, and having playdates with other mom friends. I dream about encouraging them to do what makes them happy and holding them when they are sad or scared. I dream about the house I will give them and all the things I will do to make sure it is a safe and happy place for them. A place they will be sad to leave when it is time, instead of counting down the days until they get there. Of course, there is a husband and father in this dream as well, but I have not come even slightly close to meeting the right person yet and, quite frankly, none of this is a priority at the moment. Just a dream. A dream I long for and hope to have one day in the distant future. But before I can make that dream a reality, I have to buckle down, stay focused, study hard, and get the hell out of here.

# Chapter 4

Lumberjack, or as my mother calls him, Ted, hung around for longer than I would have preferred. I did not see him often, usually only when I got home after work if he was staying the night, but when I did see him, he was drunk and almost always made me feel uncomfortable. When my mother was around, he would talk to me like I was a thirteen-year-old child. "How was school, kiddo?" he loved to say. But if she was in the bathroom or already passed out, he would show his true colors and say things like "you're beautiful just like your mom" or my personal favorite, "man, if only your mom had that ass." This one had been hard to ignore and almost had me wanting to just live in my car until graduation. *Less than six months, Emma,* I had repeated over and over in my head as I slammed my bedroom door in hopes it woke up my drunk mother, and then locked it behind me.

This was a normal nightly occurrence, me locking my bedroom door when my mother had company. Lumberjack is not the first man to hang around my mother that made me uncomfortable enough to lock my door. I have even been sleeping with a knife by my bed for as long as I can remember.

Now for the most part, the men she brought home were harmless. Losers for sure, but harmless nonetheless.

But every once in a while, there would be a man like Ted who loved to get drunk and make inappropriate comments to me. Especially once I turned fourteen and got my period. It was around this time that my curvy figure made its debut and my breasts and ass started to plump up. They would almost always wait until my mother was not around, or at least out of earshot, to make their gross comments about my tits or about how pretty I was going to be when I grew up. Thankfully, almost all of them were all talk and no bite and none of them ever laid a hand on me. But one, one got close. He's the reason I don't go to sleep unless my door is locked and my knife is on standby.

I was fifteen when Ben started hanging around the house regularly. He seemed nice and he never made me feel uncomfortable – at first. Honestly, I really enjoyed it when he came around. He would ask me how school was, play UNO with me, and cook us dinner. Even my mother was more barrable to be around when Ben was in her life. She didn't turn into a textbook, caring mom, but she did sit down for a game or two of UNO. It was the first time I had ever felt like I had a parent figure in my life.

After about four months of Ben practically living at our house, I had been getting ready for bed in my bathroom. Ben and Loraine had already gone to bed, so I did not bother closing the bathroom door. I had just finished brushing my teeth when I heard Loraine's bedroom door open. I figured one of them was getting up to get some water, as they had polished off two bottles of wine before they crashed. I did not care to run into either of them, so I waited a few seconds to see if they would pass the bathroom and then I was going to hurry to my room. But after a minute, no one passed so I quietly peeked around the bathroom door and into the hallway and that's when I saw Ben. He was walking out of my bedroom and going back into Loraine's room.

Ben didn't see me because it was nearly pitch black in the hall, but I had a nightlight in my room that shined at the doorway so I could see him well. At first, I didn't know what to think; I loved Ben, I did not want to think or assume the worst. But the longer I stood there stunned in the bathroom, the realization that he was not going into my bedroom at midnight to play UNO with me hit me like a ton of bricks, knocking the air straight out of me. Fear flooded through me and I didn't know what I was supposed to do. I obviously could not go to my mother for help. There is not a chance that she would believe me. I knew that the chances were greater of her *blaming* me somehow.

Eventually, after what felt like an eternity of me being frozen in the bathroom, I found the courage to sprint to the kitchen, grab a knife, and sprint to my room. I quickly locked it behind me and crawled under the covers, never once letting go of the knife. There was no falling asleep that night, especially after an hour later when Ben tried once again to come into my room. I remember so vividly me covering my mouth to stifle my cries and praying to God, or whoever would listen, to help me. After a few minutes, that felt like hours, he gave up trying, probably not wanting to make too much noise, and went back to my mother's room.

I was devastated. Ben was my favorite out of any man that Loraine had brought home. He made me look forward to going home after school. He made me laugh and made me feel like a normal kid for the first time ever. How could I not have seen that he was no good? I should have known better. He was with my mother, after all; of course, he was not a good man. I did not sleep for one second that night; sheer terror pulsing through my veins at every noise I heard, making it impossible to sleep. By morning, I decided I did not care if she did not believe me; I had to tell Loraine. I had to do *something.*

"Ben tried to come into my room last night," I told her the next morning the second I made sure that Ben had already left. The words left my mouth hesitantly, knowing she would either blame me or not believe me at all.

"Excuse me?" she asked with a shocked and angry tone. The anger seemed to have been directed at me though, not at Ben. That I remember well.

"I saw him go in there when I was brushing my teeth, and then he tried to open my door again an hour later, but I had locked it." At this point, I was crying. I hated crying in front of my mother, but these were tears I could not control. I was scared, and I needed my mom, but I knew I wouldn't get her.

"You're lying!" she snapped. "Go to your room!"

I did as she said and sprinted as fast as I could to my room. There were no more tears by the time I slammed my door behind me. There was not even fear. There was nothing but anger left inside me at that point. Her first instinct was not to comfort me and be angry at Ben.

Instead, she was angry at me. That is when I knew for good that I could never count on her. Ben eventually stopped coming around shortly after that. Whether it was because my mother decided to parent or not, I do not know, but from that point on, I have not fallen asleep once unless my door is locked and that same knife is on my nightstand.

# Chapter 5

There are just less than two weeks before my final semester starts and since my summer courses ended last week, I get to finally enjoy some sort of summer without worrying about school. My five-a.m. bedtime paid off because I passed that test with flying colors and ended the course with an A. Even better news: Lumberjack hasn't been over in the past couple days, so I will hopefully be able to enjoy this time without having to worry about being harassed every time I come home.

Since I do not have assignments and tests to worry about, I decide to pick up an extra couple of shifts at the coffee shop. Not much of a summer vacation, I know, but the more money I can make, the better. Which is why it is a Saturday and I am about to work a twelve-hour shift from ten a.m. to ten p.m. instead of hanging out at a pool or at the beach that is only an hour away. To be honest, I have more of a desire to make money to help go toward an apartment after I graduate than to go to dumb college parties where everyone is getting wasted and making dumb decisions. I cannot risk doing anything to prolong my fresh start. A chill coffee shop is way more my vibe anyway and Jessica will be working the later shift with me, which always makes it feel less like work and more like two friends just hanging out.

My mother is barely waking up as I am about to leave for Snaps at nine-thirty. She walks into the kitchen to pour herself a cup of the coffee that I had prepared without even a glance in my direction.

"I'm working a double shift today, so I'll be gone all day and won't be home 'til after ten," I tell her my daily plan, once again knowing she doesn't give a crap.

"Okay, well, I have a date tonight that I'm hoping goes well, so if we're hanging at the house when you get home, try not to linger around us, please."

If I had a dollar for every time she spoke a similar version of those words, I would have been able to buy my own mansion long ago.

Not lingering was going to be no problem at all because I knew I would be crashing the second I got home after a twelve-hour work day.

"Lumberjack still around?" I ask her dryly, hoping the answer is no, but that would just mean there is a *new* guy, and to be honest, Ted isn't even the worst of them, so maybe I would prefer he does stick around. Grass is always greener, right?

"His name is Ted, Emma. And no. I met someone the other day. A veterinarian, actually," she says, a smug look forming across her beautiful makeup-less face. I envy her for that. The ability to wake up and be effortlessly gorgeous.

"Really?" I ask her, genuinely surprised, because smart men who have their life together aren't my mother's usual M.O.

"Why are you so surprised?"

33

"No reason," I state as I turn around to leave. *No way this guy is legit, she has to be getting played. Wouldn't that be fun to watch? Maybe I should ask some more questions. Whatever. Not my problem.* My only concern is graduating, NOT Loraine's disastrous love life, so I push it out of my mind and head to Snaps for my double.

It's a surprisingly slow Saturday at the coffee shop. With the one hundred degrees sunny Texas weather, everyone must be wanting to be in some form of water somewhere. Even though I do think we have better iced coffee than anywhere else. I guess everyone would rather be drinking beer and seltzers on a day like today. The shift's really quite boring until Jessica shows up for the second half.

The first thing I do is tell her all about this mysterious new "vet" that my mother has somehow landed, and like always, Jessica has me cracking up every five minutes, a 180 from the boring six hours I have just had. The second shift flies by, and since I would be closing, Jessica leaves an hour before me. I love working with Jessica, but I also love closing and having an hour mostly to myself to do nothing other than mindless cleaning. I change the music to country, my favorite genre, and get busy wiping tables, cleaning coffee pots, and not thinking about anything else. It is almost like meditation and the perfect way to end a very long work day. Loraine told me to keep it down when I got home, and that would be no problem because I plan on going straight to my room to collapse on my bed. My feet and back are killing me after being on them for twelve hours straight.

When I walk in the front door shortly after ten, I'm surprised, and annoyed, to hear conversation. My mother's ridiculous cackle, which she does around the guys she brings home, booms into the living room from the kitchen. Our house is a partially open concept, and when you walk into the living room from the front door, you have the whole living area to the left and then the kitchen to the right. You can see the dining area and kitchen table, but the kitchen is behind a wall. I walk farther into the house to where I can see her and a surprisingly attractive man sitting at our dining table, each holding a glass of wine. So attractive that I find myself extremely self-conscious about my coffee-stained clothes, greasy pulled-back hair, and the bags that are most definitely under my eyes.

"Ahhh, here she is!" my mother squeals, and I legitimately turn around to see who she is talking about because it for sure as hell is not me. Did someone sneak in behind me?

"Come here, sweety!" she says again as she waves me over, looking me straight in the eyes, making me realize she is, in fact, speaking to me. I think I am in shock because I have never once in my life heard her talk to me with this kind of tone.

It takes a moment to gather my thoughts and move my feet in their direction. I walk over cautiously, not saying a word, as I observe them and try to gauge what it is that is happening right now. As I walk near them and am able to examine this man a little more closely, I realize that he may not actually be lying about being a veterinarian. He is vastly more put together than any guy she has ever brought home. His thick, dark brown hair is neat and styled a little higher on top and shorter on the sides. He is sitting down, but I can tell he has a taller build – at least six feet – and he is wearing a button-down tucked into a pair of fitted blue jeans with tan loafers and a Rolex on his left wrist. He runs a hand through his hair and seems almost nervous as I finally make my way to them, and it makes him look young. There is no way he is older than thirty, let alone older than my mother.

"Honey, this is Jay. Jay Rowan! Jay, this is my wonderful daughter, Emma!" she exclaims.

Sweety, honey, and wonderful are words my mother has never used toward me, so I can barely even manage a "nice to meet you" as I reach out to shake Jay's hand. My mother's performance has left me speechless. But when his hand makes contact with mine, it awakens something in me. The sensation of his skin on mine sends a shock wave down to my toes that jerks me back to reality.

Holy crap. What was that? Who is this guy? This is not the type of guy my mother brings home. This is an extremely attractive man that clearly has his life together, and I feel anger rip through my chest. Why is he here with my mother, who is trying to act like some sort of perfect mom that has literally never existed? I thought this man was going to be playing her, but it turns out I was completely wrong. She is the one playing him.

"So, your mom tells me you work at a coffee shop?" he asks with seemingly genuine curiosity; all traces of nervousness I thought I saw earlier have disappeared from his face. He seems cool and collected and very laid back.

"Uh yah, I also am about to graduate a semester early with a major in Communications," I say dryly. Enraged, but not surprised, that my mother left out a pretty important detail about me. In her defense, she probably does not even know what my major is or where I even go to school, to be honest. The only reason she knows I work at a coffee shop is because I have brought home coffee for her before.

"Wow, that's awesome, Emma. You seem to be an extremely hard worker; that's impressive," he compliments me.

No one has ever encouraged me or complimented me like this before, besides Jessica, and even though he is here on a date with my mother, the look he gives me as he says those words makes me wish I would have thrown on at least *some* makeup this morning. My skin is bare, my long brown hair is up in a high bun on my head, and I am feeling pretty damn plain in my black fitted T-shirt and mom jeans. Especially as I stand next to Loraine, whose blonde, shiny hair is curled perfectly and hanging over her shoulders. She has a stunning pink jumpsuit and white wedges on, paired with perfect rosy cheeks and smoky eyes. I feel damn near invisible as I stand next to her and I try hard to ignore the self-doubt that is trying to creep in.

I do not like to physically compare myself to Loraine because I know that I can also look stunning. Just not right now in my wrinkly work clothes. But I try hard to pull forth my usual confidence and carry on with my conversation with Jay.

"So, you're a vet?" I ask him curiously, paying

attention to every detail on his face to see if I can see any hint of a lie.

"Yep, graduated from the College of Veterinary Medicine at Texas A&M University about three years ago, worked for a couple of different veterinarians after that, and finally opened up my own practice about a year ago," he says proudly but without any hint of gloating, and from what I can tell, there are no signs of deceit.

Assuming he started college at the normal age of eighteen, and from my understanding of veterinary school, that would make my assumption that he can't be over thirty correct. I am curious, though, at his exact age, and although I am dying to ask him, it would come off as strange, so I don't. Is Loraine taking a crack at the gold-digging life? For a moment, I am impressed that she finally has some higher standards for herself, but then I remember that she is completely full of shit right now and is very clearly giving this man a version of herself that does not exist.

"Wow, that's awesome!" I tell him, returning the enthusiasm he gave me just moments ago.

"Yes, y'all are both amazing! Well, honey, I'm sure you're tired after your long day; why don't you head to bed?" she tells me, but I can hear the annoyance in her voice. Jay, who doesn't know her like I do, probably can't hear it at all, but I have heard it for long enough that I know it is there, peeking through the chipper tone she is trying to fool him with. I have served my purpose of making her look like a caring, doting mother, but now I am interrupting her date, and she is telling me it is time to go.

"Nice to meet you." I wave at him, and he returns the

gesture.

"You too, Emma," he says, and I can't stop the shiver that climbs up my spine and trickles behind my ears at the sound of my name on his lips.

My plan to pass out the minute I hit the pillow flies out the window because for the next hour, I hear my mother and Jay flirting and laughing in the kitchen, and for some reason, unbeknownst to me, it makes me absolutely livid.

Finally, around midnight, I hear them both go into her room and shut the door. I roll on my back and groan, feeling so unsettled by the thought of them in her room together. But why? She has done this night after night, but for some reason, the thought of them two in her bed haunts me. Maybe it's because he seems like a decent man who does not deserve to be lied to. Or maybe it's the look he gave me as he praised my work ethic. I don't know, but I do know that I do not like this feeling. I turn my white noise machine up as loud as it will go to ensure I don't hear anything I don't want to, and I toss and turn the rest of the night.

# CHAPTER 6

"How are Loraine and Hotty Vet? Are they still together?" Jessica asks, hoping for some juicy gossip.

"Yep. Somehow, she has managed to make herself seem like this amazing woman and mother. I seriously can't handle it. I found out last night, as I was eavesdropping on their conversation in the living room, that she told him she is a retired lawyer! A retired lawyer! Can you believe that?" I snort.

"You're kidding me!" Jessica exclaims as she wipes down a table, all eyes turning to her after her loud, shocked response. "Sorry," she whispers to them quickly, and I can't help but laugh.

My last semester of school has finally started, and it has been a month since my mother brought Jay home. They seem to still be going steady, and he still seems to be believing this persona she has put on. He has spent quite a few nights over at our house, and my mother has actually spent some at his as well. I relish in these nights of having the house to myself. Every time he is over, he is always extremely nice and seems genuinely interested in talking with me, but it is not long before my mother turns the conversation back to her or convinces him to go to bed with her.

I have probably only spoken to him for a total of thirty

minutes over the past month, but it has been enough to tell me that he is a normal and decent guy that does not deserve to be played by Loraine. Never in my life have I cared about her dating life until now, and I am still not quite sure why I care so much. Maybe it's because I think Jay is too good for her, and watching her manipulate him seems to get under my skin more than anything else my mother has done. I find myself itching for graduation to be here more than ever.

"I just can't believe he's falling for it. He seems so smart," I state.

"Well, from what you've told me about your mom, she needs validation from men, so the fact that she's pulled a hot ass vet, five years younger than her, is probably boosting her ego to the freaking moon. I'm sure she's going to do whatever it takes to keep him around, including pretending to be a decent human," she explains so clearly that it all makes perfect sense.

"That's very true. God, Jessica, I wish you could see him, though. He is seriously perfect. Perfect hair. Perfect smile. The way he seems to genuinely care about whatever you're saying. He is literally the perfect man, and I can't believe she has pulled him. She doesn't deserve him," I say, getting lost in my words, not realizing what exactly I was saying.

"Oh. My God!" Jessica whispers as she walks back behind the counter, staring at me with a shocked look on her face.

"What?" I ask her, confused.

"You're into him! You're into your mother's

boyfriend!" she shrieks.

"What? I am absolutely not into Jay," I assure her.

"Did you just hear yourself, Emma? You were practically drooling as you were talking about how perfect he is! Perfect hair, perfect smile! You are SO into him!" she exclaims.

Unable to respond or refute, I stare at her, stunned. Is that why I am feeling this anger and annoyance toward the whole situation? Am I jealous of my mother for being with Jay? I mean, he is gorgeous, and every time he speaks to me, my whole body seems to buzz, and I can still feel the way my hand tingled when he shook it a month ago. Shit.

"Holy shit," I mumble.

"Uh, YAH! Holy shit is right. I mean, I don't blame you; if he is as hot as you say he is, I'm pissed off too that your mother has landed him."

I laugh at that, relieved because Jessica doesn't make me feel embarrassed; she just immediately validates my feelings. She always knows exactly what to say to make me feel better when I need it.

"I barely know him, so it's not like I want to be with him. I guess I am just pissed that my mother may get a happy ending she doesn't deserve." I sigh.

Jessica turns sympathetic and grabs my hand. "Hey, in almost four months, it won't be any of your worry and concern anymore; you'll get to start fresh with a new life and make your own happy ending!" She reassures me.

"You're right. They aren't my concern. Graduating and moving on with my life is the only thing I should be focusing on right now," I say matter-of-factly.

It's Jessica's night to close the shop, but I stay with her and help so we can go get a drink afterward at a local bar. Knowing that I now have these weird jealous feelings about my mother's boyfriend makes me want to be anywhere but my house. Jessica threw out the idea of grabbing a drink, and I quickly took her up on it. Jessica and I don't really hang out outside of work because I am always super busy with school, and although I do need to study, a girls' night sounds way better and way more necessary at the moment.

It's almost midnight, and after lots of laughs and two margaritas, I'm pulling onto my street feeling a lot more relaxed. That is, until I see Jay's pickup truck parked in his usual spot in the driveway. Part of me was hoping they were at his place so I could just sleep in peace. But another part of me, a very stupid part of me, is glad to see it parked there. Hesitantly, I get out of my car and hope that my mother and her boyfriend are not flirting in the kitchen or, even worse, being loud in her bedroom. I've heard my mom having sex with many men, and now that I know where my feelings lie when it comes to Jay, I'm not sure I could take hearing them have sex. The thought alone makes me want to vomit. Typically, my mother passes out drunk by ten p.m. at the latest, but with this new facade she has put on over the last month, I really don't know what I am going to walk into these days. I still cannot believe she has made it this long without her normal drinking.

I enter the house and my shoulders slump in relief as I hear nothing but silence. The anxious pulsing that was raging through my whole body slows, and I relax as I head to the kitchen for a glass of water. It immediately starts up again after just a few steps when I see Jay sitting alone at the kitchen table, drinking what looks like tea and scrolling through his phone. He is sitting in nothing but pajama pants, and I can see every detail of muscle throughout his arms and abs. He isn't bulky, but instead lean and toned. My heart races even faster as my eyes graze down his bare chest. I can feel the heat rising to my cheeks. There is definitely no denying my attraction to him anymore. I can feel the desire I have for him deep in the pit of my stomach just by looking at him.

It's dark in the house and he must have not heard me walk in because he doesn't notice me admiring him. I clear my throat to let him know that I'm here, and when he looks up at me, I swear I see his eyes flicker quickly to my chest and then back to my eyes. It was less than a millisecond, but there's no denying it happened, and I have to hide the smirk that my mouth wants to make. Thank God I had this top still in my car from a date I went on a while back with a man named Dave. I ended up sleeping over at his house that night, and I slept in a pair of his sweats. He let me wear the sweats home, and even though I am sure it's weird, I still wear them often because they are insanely comfortable and probably more expensive than my nicest items of clothing. The top I wore on that date had gotten left in my car, and that's where it had stayed until tonight, when I threw it on before Jessica and I went to grab drinks. So, as I stand here now in front of Jay, I am not in my nasty coffee-stained work T-shirt but in a black silk cami with lace lining the top and since my strapless bra is making my C-cup breasts push together, my cleavage is busting out of the lace perfectly. I feel sexy and confident. Even more so now, knowing that Jay has checked me out.

"Emma, hey, how are you?" he asks, seeming a little uncomfortable that it's just the two of us in the kitchen and he's wearing nothing but pajama pants. And probably because he also just blatantly checked out my tits.

"Hey, I'm good. I went out after work, so I'm just getting some water to hydrate," I say as I head to the cabinets to grab a glass. My hands are trembling slightly at being alone with him in this close proximity and I force them to steady as I reach to grab a glass from the cabinet.

"Nice, sounds fun; I miss the college days," he states.

"Oh, I don't do this often, if ever, because of work and school, but my coworker knew I needed to relax so she convinced me," I say, correcting him.

"Really? That's a shame; going out with your friends is what college is all about," he shares, and I cringe just a bit, knowing that is something I have had to sacrifice in order to get out of here.

"Yah, well, not everyone is having to pay for their college with their own money. I also have goals that I want to achieve and graduating as soon as I can is how I get them. So, unfortunately, partying can't be a priority for me." I'm trying to not sound bitter when I say this, but his comment sparked something sour inside me.

"You're paying for college all on your own? What about your mom's money she saved from her career as a lawyer or the money your grandparents left?" he asks, seeming genuinely confused.

I let out a sigh, unsure if I should tell him everything he doesn't know. I want to. I *really* want to, and it takes everything in me not to word vomit all the lies Loraine has told him. But ultimately, it's not my place, and he should find out the truth about my mother all on his own.

"I don't know; I just know it wasn't enough money to pay for my college, so here I am," I say, not necessarily throwing my mother under the bus, but hopefully planting some questions and concerns in his head.

"Oh. Well, that's a shame, you really should be able to enjoy yourself some more right now. So, what are your goals? What's your plan after you graduate?"

It shouldn't, but the effort he's putting into having an actual conversation with me is exciting. Too exciting. I remind myself, as I take a sip of my water, that he is my *mother's* boyfriend. But the thrill of it takes over and before I know it, I'm sitting down in the chair across from him at the table.

"I'd like to find a job in marketing or maybe sales and then move into my own place."

"Nice. Do you wanna stay here in Houston?" he asks.

"I will go anywhere I can as long as I can have my own place," I say too quickly, probably confusing him but hopefully sparking more questions underneath that luscious hair.

He stares at me for a few seconds with scrutinizing eyes. My cheeks burn, and my palms sweat with his eyes on me like this because it feels almost intimate at this moment. Him with his shirt off, me in my low-cut top, the lights dimmed. Does he look at Loraine like this? *God, don't think about that, Emma.*

Dying to change the subject because I can't handle his eyes on me any longer, I ask the question I have been wanting to know since we met, "How old are you if you don't mind me asking?" I hope he doesn't take offense to this, but I need to know.

"I'm twenty-eight," he answers, unfazed by my question. Although it shouldn't, it relieves me to know that he is closer to my age than he is to my mother's.

"What about you?" he asks.

"Twenty-one." Maybe I'm going crazy, or maybe it's the margaritas, but I swear I see his eyes flicker down to my breasts once again as I answer him. It was the quickest of movements, not as quick as the first but still barely noticeable.

"And your birthday?" My heart clenches at the way he seems to really want to know more about me.

"December twelfth," I tell him, and then ask him the same.

"May fourth," he answers.

And then I say quite possibly the most embarrassing thing I have ever said in my entire life. "May the fourth be with you." I cringe and shake my head, immediately regretting it, but Jay laughs. A genuine laugh. And the embarrassment floats away and I find it easy to laugh along with him. He checks the time on his phone when the laughter stops, and I panic.

"So, it's pretty awesome that you own your own veterinary practice," I tell him before he can get up and go to my mother's bed.

"Oh yah, thanks, I'm pretty proud of it. It's definitely been an exciting year," he says as his eyes move off his phone screen and back to me.

"What made you want to become a vet?" I ask him.

His mouth forms into a perfect grin, showing off his perfect white teeth and a perfect dimple that forms on his right cheek. My heart throbs. "My dad. My parents have a farm and my dad especially loved animals. On top of taking care of our farm animals, he was always bringing home stray dogs and cats and even bunnies and some reptiles. He didn't go to college and worked as a mechanic, but his love for animals is who he was, and he imprinted that love on me as well. He died when I was in high school, and I knew that I was going to follow both of our dreams and become a veterinarian. For him."

I have to blink back the tears that begin to sting my eyes before he can see them. The way he talks about his father makes me extremely emotional. I can hear his love for him just from the words he uses. What that must feel like. "Wow. I'm so sorry about your father, but it sounds like he would be pretty damn proud of you," I assure him.

"Thanks, I don't hear that often. It feels good." He chuckles, and I feel immediate irritation at my mother because I know for a fact, she hasn't asked him any of this. I am sure this is something he would like to talk about with her, and she probably has no idea about any of it.

"Your mom hasn't mentioned anything about your dad, are you close?" he asks.

I laugh internally at his question, and it just adds more

clarification to the fact that they probably do not have many meaningful conversations, if at all.

"No, I don't know him or anything about him."

"Really? Your mom didn't tell you anything?" he asks, surprised.

"Nope, apparently he left her the minute he found out she was pregnant at fifteen and she never saw him again." Wow, how did I end up with the world's worst parents? Our stories are night and day, and it's hard to ignore the jealousy I feel. The relationship he shared with his father, although devastatingly short, is one I've only dreamt about.

"Wow. I'm so sorry, Emma. That has to be tough. At least you have your mom," he tells me, as if that is a good thing.

His comment was intended to be helpful, but it only makes me sick and I can barely respond to it. It isn't his fault, I know that. He's being played and doesn't know any better. But this only makes me more upset. This conversation is too much. I grab my water and stand up from the table, unable to look him in the eye any longer. Unable to handle the way this conversation is making me feel.

"Yah, well, I'm exhausted, so I'm gonna head to bed. Goodnight, Jay." I turn away quickly, hoping he doesn't sense the shift in my mood. But of course, he does.

"Are you okay? Did I say something?" he asks with concern.

"I'm fine," I reply as I swallow the lump in my throat. I barely manage a "night" and quickly head off to my room, not even bothering to brush my teeth or wash my face.

I don't cry often; in fact, I would say I'm pretty tough. I have built a thick skin over the years, but that conversation with Jay set me off and opened up something in me that I like to keep closed. His relationship with his dad made me feel sorry for his loss but also sorry for mine because it's nothing I have ever experienced with a parent and never will. Mourning something I've never had but always yearned for hits me like a ton of bricks. That, combined with my new feelings for Jay, something else I will never have, has me crying myself to sleep for the first time in my adult life.

# CHAPTER 7

The next morning, my eyes burn as if they've been rinsed with boiling water. I don't need to look in a mirror to see that they probably look like marshmallows with pupils on them. I'm not sure I've cried like that since I was a little girl and my mother had left me alone during a bad thunderstorm. I was probably only eight years old, and Loraine had been gone, assumingly on a date, when a terrible storm hit. Thunder rattled so loud the house shook, and I hid under my covers, sobbing until I heard the front door finally open after what seemed like an eternity. I ran straight to her, wrapped my arms around her waist, and cried into her stomach, soaking her satin top with my tears. "Ugh, Emma, god, grow up," she told me as she unwrapped my arms from her waist and went straight to her room, shutting the door behind her.

This memory guts me. Oh, how I wish I could hug that little girl myself. But I can't, so instead I wrap my arms around me right now. "You're a strong ass bitch, Emma. Less than four months. You can do this," I say out loud as I give myself the love and comfort I needed all those years ago.

It's six-thirty a.m. when I roll out of bed to get ready for my eight a.m. comm theory class. My heart, still a tender mess from every emotion that I felt last night. Jay opening up to me about his relationship with his father brought up feelings that I have avoided for a long time. I have longed for a relationship like that, and even though it just isn't in the cards for Loraine and I, and it's not even something I want with *her*, it still stings.

Slowly making my way across my room to head to the bathroom to freshen up, I open my bedroom door and run smack into something warm and sturdy. Incredibly sturdy. Jay.

Just as shirtless as he had been last night. My insides tingle at the sight of him and goosebumps cover my skin at the contact of his skin with mine. Oh man, I'm in trouble.

He grabs me by the shoulders to steady me so I don't fall. "Shit, sorry, Emma."

My lips are incapable of forming a complete sentence; the only thing grabbing my focus are his hands on my skin and his eyes that roam over my entire body. I instantly become aware of my bare legs in my tiny pajama shorts and my nipples that are poking through my white tank top.

"Oh no, it was my fault. Sorry, Jay," I mumble as I try to maneuver around him in the hall to get to the bathroom door. To break up this moment that has me wanting to squirm out of my skin.

"Emma, wait." He grabs my elbow gently, but with enough force to stop me from moving any farther away from him.

I turn around and can't help but notice every detail of his seemingly sculpted body. The toned muscles, the multiple freckles he has, and a scar at least two inches long on the left side of his abdomen, right next to his belly button. It takes everything in me not to reach out and graze my finger over it.

"Please tell me if I said something last night that upset you," he says, concern etched on his face, breaking me from my trance.

"No, Jay, really. I'm fine," I say, not having the energy or desire to think about it anymore, although I know he can probably tell I am not fine since I'm sure my eyes are a red and puffy mess.

"You're not; I heard you crying last night." His thumb, still lingering on my elbow, rubs over my skin so slightly that I think I may have imagined it, but that doesn't stop the hunger that roars through me. The throbbing that forms just below my belly button.

My eyes shut, and I let out a long breath, trying to shake off the effect he has on me and the embarrassment that forms at the thought of him hearing me cry. I don't like coming off as weak. How did he even hear me? I may have been crying like a baby, but I tried to stay quiet.

"I don't want to talk about it, and you don't need to worry about me, Jay."

"I'm finding that hard to do right now." His head lowers closer to mine, no more than an inch, but enough to make me weak in the knees.

His eyes stare into mine, his fingers now grasping my arm even tighter than before, and his thumb is rubbing over my skin now. A sensation explodes through me under his touch that tells me there is no way that I'm imagining this. I see him glance down to my chest, but unlike last night, he lets his eyes linger just long enough, which tells me it was no accident. His eyes come back up to meet mine again and there is something happening. Something in this moment between us that is intensifying as each second goes by, becoming too much for me to handle.

"I'm fine, Jay," I snap, knowing he doesn't deserve the harshness but also knowing it is the only way I can end this moment before something happens that we both regret. I turn around quickly and lock myself in the bathroom before he can stop me.

My body and mind feel drained from crying all night, and now even more so from the confusing way my body reacted to Jay's fingers on my skin. The way his eyes smoldered as they lingered on my breasts. What on earth is going through his head? I know I didn't imagine his eyes on me; the way my nipples are still tingling tells me without a doubt that he was looking at them. I know there is no way he didn't feel the connection we just had. But I also know that he just slept in my mother's bed.

But even despite this, I can't stop the heat that builds between my thighs as I think about the way he looked at me. I can't stop the wetness that forms inside me as I think about his hands on my skin. I can't think about anything other than *him*, and I don't stop my fingers as they make their way to do the only thing that will take the edge off. The only thing that will take my mind off whatever just happened. A quiet moan escapes me as my fingers roll over my nipples. I pinch them both with the tips of my fingers and moan again as I imagine it's Jay's fingers instead of my own. One hand releases my breast and I slowly move it downward to where the throbbing has intensified. When my fingers make contact with my swollen flesh, I bite my lip and pinch my nipple even harder. The speed of my fingers increases as I imagine Jay in here with me, my nipple between his teeth, his fingers rubbing circles where I am now, and I have to bite my lip even harder to stifle my cry as I climax and the waves rush through me.

"Great," I mutter to myself as I realize I just masturbated to my mother's boyfriend.

My classes end around noon today, so I work the midday shift at the coffee shop. Jessica is off today, so I don't even have her to take my mind off everything that has happened with Jay since last night, and it is all I can think about during my shift. We were basically complete strangers yesterday and now there is this strange new connection between the two of us. And on top of it all, he is dating my mother. What am I doing? No, what is *he* doing?

Refusing to go home after my shift since it is only five p.m., I head back to campus, picking up some Chinese food on the way, and then head to the library to study the rest of the night away.

It's almost midnight by the time I get home, and once again, I can't tell if I'm thrilled or devastated when I see Jay's truck in the driveway. The fact that he is here, and is here almost daily, means he and my mother are moving quickly. Which I hate. But in my own selfish way, I'm glad he is here. I want to see him again. To talk to him. To figure out what is going on between us. Which is why I'm praying he is up and my mother is not.

To my relief, I see Jay sitting alone in the kitchen, reading a book with a mug of tea. An utterly ridiculous amount of excitement surges through me at the sight of him. I also notice an almost empty bottle of vodka on the counter, and to my surprise, I feel glad at the sight of it. To know that my mother is back to her normal drinking and that she is hopefully one step closer to showing Jay her true colors.

"Hi," I say as I drop my backpack on the floor and head to the table. It isn't even a question that I'm going to sit down with him.

"Hey. How was your day?" He is hesitant, I can tell, after our interaction this morning.

"Same as usual. School, work, study. What about you?" I ask with an upbeat tone, trying to show him that I am in a better mood than I was this morning. My morning shower definitely helped.

"Uh, it was pretty rough, actually. I had to put down a nine-year-old lab. He was a good boy. Days like these are always tough."

"Oh my gosh, Jay. I can't imagine; I'm so sorry. His poor owners, I bet that was awful." I don't know what it is like to even have a pet, let alone lose one, but I can imagine it sucks. I asked Loraine for a dog so many times growing up because I needed a companion. I would see dogs on television shows and movies, and they added so much joy to their owners' lives and I wanted that more than anything, but Loraine shut the idea down time after time. That would have been more money spent on something that wasn't hers.

Jay just nods his head and takes a sip of his tea. I can tell it is not easy for him to talk about, and I find myself wanting to make him feel better. To try to think of a way to help him get his mind off it. So, I ask him, "Do you have any funny vet stories?"

"Oh man, so many!" He laughs and I can see some spark come back into his eyes. For the next hour, he proceeds to tell me about a turtle named Kevin that would always get rose thorns stuck in his face because he was so obsessed with his owner's rose bush; a cat named Tessa that could sit, shake, and fetch like a dog, and a parrot that told him to fuck off every time he came in.

We're both cracking up as he finishes recounting all of the funny memories from his job, and I can tell his whole mood has shifted. I hope that I have a career someday that I am as passionate about as Jay is about being a vet. Right now, I am just passionate about graduating and getting away from here.

"Did y'all ever have any pets?" he asks.

"No, but I've always wanted a Golden Retriever," I answer him.

He smiles at that answer. "Good choice. They're always my favorite patients." And then he seems to get a look in his eyes as if he's remembering something and then that look turns to confusion.

"What is it?" I ask because the look is so obvious it'd be weird not to acknowledge it.

"It's nothing. Well, I don't know. It's just, on my first date with your mom, she told me she'd always wanted a dog and then when I asked her why y'all never had one, she told me you were allergic. At least I think she did, but maybe I misheard her." He shakes his head as if trying to pull that memory to the forefront of his mind.

Heat rises to my cheeks that have to be beet red right now. Unbelievable! I'm in such shock it takes me minutes to gather my thoughts and say something.

"I'm not allergic. I've always wanted a dog; I asked her for one many times and she always said no," I tell him, not caring at all if it makes Loraine look bad.

"Hmmm. Maybe you were allergic when you were little then? And you just don't remember," he says, trying to come up with a logical explanation for the confusion.

"No. Never." It comes off sharp, and I don't mean it to. It's not directed at him, but it's impossible to hide my irritated tone.

"Maybe I misheard her then," he states, and I know we'll never know the answer because I'm sure as hell not going to tell Loraine her boyfriend and I are having late-night chats, and I'm sure he won't be telling her either.

He changes the subject and starts telling me about other dog breeds he loves that make great pets, and I try to go back to the mood I was in before I knew about the lie Loraine told, but it's difficult.

By the time we both finally head to bed, it is almost two in the morning and as I lie under my covers, unable to sleep, I go over our conversation in my head and wonder to myself if he had told my mother about the bad day he had. I hate myself for comparing my relationship with Jay to my mother's relationship with him. How sick and twisted is that? I force myself to put them both out of my mind so I can try to find some sleep. I have a big test tomorrow and *that* is what I need to be focusing on. Not Jay. Not whatever relationship I'm conjuring up in my head. But as I shut my eyes tighter, begging for sleep to take over, I think about Loraine telling Jay I was allergic to dogs and I toss and turn in anger the rest of the night.

# CHAPTER 8

Over the course of the next week, Jay and I continue to have many late-night kitchen talks. Or "after-hours chats" as I like to call them. It's always close to midnight by the time I get home from either the library or my shift at Snaps, and so far, every day this week, Jay has been at the kitchen table when I walk in the door. He is always reading a book or scrolling through his phone, and it feels as if he is waiting for me. But I know that can't be the case. He must just be a night owl like myself. Either way, I stupidly relish in each of these secret moments with him. They are nothing but amiable, but I feel as if I know Jay better than I know anyone. Not that I know many people. But he has shared a lot more about his family, especially his relationship with his mother, since his dad passed away. How the tragedy has brought them even closer. I have to bite my tongue from telling him how jealous I am of that. How lucky he is to have her.

I tell Jay as much as I can about my life without going into the gritty details despite every ounce of me wanting to explode with the truth. But I am still set on Jay finding out about the type of person my mother really is all on his own. It takes everything in me not to ask him about their relationship. What do they do every evening before I get home? What do they talk about? How did they meet? What is she like when it's just the two of them? What is she doing that is making him stick around for so damn long? I can't imagine it. I can't imagine my mother having a meaningful conversation with anyone, let alone someone like Jay. Someone who is caring and passionate.

It kills me that he is still with her. But at the same time, I have gotten so used to these moments with him that the thought of him not being here every night when I come home kills me more.

What I do know is that the longer their relationship goes on, the harder it is getting for my mother to hide her true colors. It's not often I'm around the both of them, so I don't know what she is saying to him, but I do know that the empty wine and vodka bottles are increasing each week, and I wonder what Jay thinks about that. Does he think that she is just enjoying a glass or two after a long day, or does he realize she probably started drinking long before he even comes over?

There is a lot I want to know about their relationship, but I have to keep reminding myself every day that it is *their* relationship. It is none of my business, and the more I get involved, the more off track of my goal I'm becoming. In just over three months, I will be out of here, and that should be the only thing I'm focused on. But when I come home and find Jay sitting alone at the kitchen table every night, it is nearly impossible for me not to join him. And the more that I get to know him, the more it feels like his relationship *is* my business.

He has been here just about every night for the past month. There were nights at the very beginning of their relationship where my mother didn't come home, making me assume they were staying at his place, but that stopped a while ago. Now he stays here at least five times a week. He is a single veterinarian, I am sure he has a nice home. Why is he here all the time? Just another thing to add to my list of things I want to ask him about but can't. So instead, we spend these secret moments solely getting to know one another. We share our love for good coffee. What our favorite movies and shows are. What my classes this semester are like and which of his patients are his favorite.

These moments with him become what I look forward to every day, so when I walk in the house after a very busy Sunday night at the coffee shop and don't find Jay sitting at the table, I find myself completely devastated. Especially because his truck is here. It's in the driveway right next to Loraine's, where it always is. But his chair at the table that I've grown so used to finding him in sits empty. I stand alone in the kitchen, silence ringing in my ears as my heart shatters into a million pieces. Jay not being at this table right now can only mean one thing.

He is in my mother's room with her. Obviously, I know they have slept together, but it's not something I let myself think about, especially since he is always in the kitchen when I get home. I try to force the thought out of my head but I wasn't prepared for how this would make me feel. For how close I hadn't realized I had become with Jay. I think about leaving, but I am past the point of exhaustion and I tell myself that I will go to bed and leave first thing in the morning before they wake up. I don't want to see him. If he didn't want to talk to me tonight, then fine, but I won't give him another chance to. I'll sleep for a few hours and be gone before the sun comes up.

I head to the bathroom to get ready for bed and do everything in my power to push down the hurt that's consuming me, knowing Jay chose my mother tonight instead of me. But why wouldn't he? She's his girlfriend, not me.

I'm standing in front of the sink, brushing my teeth, when I hear it.

Moaning.

The blood drains from my face. Bile rises up my throat. The toothbrush falls from my trembling fingers, making a loud thud in the sink but continues to vibrate. I turn the water off and grab my noisy toothbrush so I can hear better. So I can make sure I am hearing what I think I'm hearing. It's dreadfully clear and torture to my ears. I can hear Jay's deep grunts and my mother's moans, as what I can only assume is him fucking her, and I have to grasp onto the counter to stop myself from collapsing to the ground.

The thought of them together like that, naked and intertwined, wrecks me. I can physically feel my heart being ripped apart in my chest, and all I want is to make it go away. Not even bothering to take off my clothes, I turn the shower on and sit in the tub, letting the water pour over me, drowning out any noises coming from my mother's room. And then I cry. I cry hard because now I know what's happening between Jay and me. Now I know that I am in love with my mother's boyfriend.

# CHAPTER 9

Once again, I am physically and mentally drained. This is apparently the new normal for me. After hearing Jay and my mother having sex a week ago, I have avoided my house entirely. Which means I'm at the library studying until I know that Jay won't be in the kitchen when I get home. And based on the times I have spent there with him, I can't go home until at least two in the morning. And since I would usually see him in the mornings since we wake up at the same time for school and work, I have to wake up even earlier so I can avoid him. I've thought about just sleeping at the library numerous times, but I can't be walking around campus and Snaps unshowered with dirty clothes. So basically, I'm surviving on three to four hours of sleep every night. Thank God I work at a coffee shop.

"You look like shit," Jessica tells me.

It's one of those weird weeks where our work schedules don't align and it's the first time Jessica and I are seeing each other since what happened. I want more than anything to be able to tell Jessica what happened, but can I admit out loud to another human that I'm in love with my mother's boyfriend?

"Yah, it's been a shit week," I say as I put the lid on the vanilla latte I just finished making. I grab the counter with both hands and let my head fall because carrying all of this alone is becoming too much to handle.

"Hey, Emma, what's going on?" Jessica rests her hand on my back. The touch is soothing, and it feels good to know I have a friend, so I decide to tell her.

"I can't get into it now but maybe we can grab a coffee after work?" I ask her.

"Of course," she tells me.

After our shift ends at four, we order our favorite cappuccinos and cozy up in one of the booths. As embarrassing as it is to speak the words out loud, I tell her everything. The minute I finish getting it all out, I know I did the right thing. I don't necessarily feel better, but it does feel like a weight has been lifted.

"Wow." She takes a sip of her warm drink as she processes everything I just unloaded on her.

"I know. I really, like *really,* need these next few months to fly by."

"So, do you think he, like, purposefully waits up for you? It seems like he enjoys these conversations just as much as you do," she questions.

"I wonder that too. But maybe that's his thing. Maybe he's just a night owl and is up late even at his own place? Well, whenever he stays there, which doesn't seem like a lot. I don't know, it's all so confusing," I respond.

"Yah, why not go home then? He doesn't have to stay at y'all's place after your mom goes to sleep. Especially since you said he leaves before your mom even wakes up. Very interesting." Her eyes crease like she's trying to find all the answers to this incredibly weird situation.

"Yah, it's all so weird. It did seem like he enjoyed our

talks, but he had to have known I'd hear them; they were being so loud, and he knows I stay up late. I feel like I read our relationship all wrong; he's clearly enjoying being with my mother. I mean, you don't make *those* noises unless you're enjoying yourself." I wince as I say it, the moans and grunts coming back to me.

We're interrupted by a clearing of a throat and look over to see one of our regulars, a senior named Landon, standing next to our booth. He attends another college in the area so we don't see each other often besides here at work, but he's come by enough that I wouldn't call him a stranger anymore. We've flirted back and forth quite a bit at the coffee shop over the last couple years, and it's very obvious he's into me with how many times he's subtly checked me out while ordering drinks. But to my surprise, he has never made a move, so neither did I. I barely have enough time to date as it is so unless a guy makes the first move, I don't waste my time.

"Hey, Emma; hey, Jessica!" he says, completely oblivious to the kind of conversation he just interrupted.

"Hey Landon, what's up?" I ask him, trying to sound nice but also wanting to get him out of here as fast as I can so I can get back to this very important and therapeutic conversation with Jessica.

"I was wondering, Emma, if you'd like to grab a drink with me tonight?" he asks with a surprising amount of confidence, seeing as how both Jessica and I were obviously having a serious conversation and I am not really giving him my full attention. He has had years to ask me out and he is choosing this exact moment to finally do it? Talk about poor timing. If he had asked this a month ago, I would probably have said yes. His buzz cut paired with the perfect amount of stubble on his face do work well together, and he is extremely nice to look at. But now I'm in love with my mother's boyfriend. There is just no way my mind could handle anything else right now.

"Oh, wow. Landon, thanks for asking, but…"

"She'd love to!" Jessica exclaims, like it's not weird at all that she is accepting a date on my behalf. I look at her like she has completely lost her mind. Clearly, she *has* lost her mind. Does she not remember all the things I just told her?

She continues, "We had plans tonight, so that's why she was going to say no, but I have a big test coming up, so I really should study anyway. Emma, you should *totally* go." She emphasizes the "totally" and gives me a look with her eyes, like I am supposed to know what she's doing.

"Emma? What do you think?" Landon questions hopefully, clearly wanting clarification from me because he is finally realizing that he has interrupted a very weird moment.

I think about it for a second but realize Jessica seems to have a plan and maybe I should just go along with it. I can get his number and always cancel later if I need to.

"Uh yah, sure, that sounds good," I say as I sip my latte, trying to cover up the fact that I would rather say no.

"Great! What's your number?" He pulls out his phone.

I give him my number, and he tells me that he will text me so we can hash out the details of our date, and then he leaves.

"Jessica, what the hell?" I proclaim.

"Emma, this is a perfect chance to see if your feelings for Jay are one-sided! Have Landon come pick you up tonight and make sure Jay knows you're going on a date, and see how he reacts! If he reacts jealous in any way, then you know you aren't the only one who's feeling a connection," she says with a smile spread across her face, clearly very proud of her plan.

Thinking about it for a second, I realize that even though I don't really want to go on a date with Landon, it's not the worst idea to try and figure out what is going on with Jay. I mean, is it fair to Landon? No. And is it crazy that I am trying to make my mother's boyfriend jealous? Absolutely. But I am desperate at this point to figure out what is going on in Jay's head.

Three hours later, I'm in my bathroom getting ready for my date with Landon. We decided he would pick me up here at eight p.m. and we would go grab a drink at a local bar. My bathroom door is open because I want it to be obvious that I'm getting ready for something, and I can hear my mother and Jay in the kitchen eating dinner, my mother talking about her hair appointment. I roll my eyes because I bet she hasn't even asked him how his day was. This is my first time being home and near the two of them in almost two weeks, and I'm dying to know if Jay has been wondering where I've been. I haven't seen him yet because I was in my room when I heard him come in. I can hear the two of them laughing, and it takes everything in me not to just grab my stuff and get out of here. But that's not part of the plan. I need to know if I'm crazy or if something is actually going on between Jay and me, so I push the nausea down and finish applying my mascara.

My makeup and hair are finally done, so I head to my room to pick out an outfit and settle on a thin-strap pastel pink crop top with my favorite distressed mom jeans and black strappy heels. There is a new chill in the air because it's now October, so I throw on my black leather jacket and decide on a pair of silver hoops to throw it all together.

I grab my purse and head to the bathroom for one last check before I head to the kitchen, where Jay will finally see me for the first time in what feels like forever. My heart grows heavy, and my insides feel as if they're twisting together into knots. I haven't seen his face since before I heard them having sex, and I miss it. I miss the small dimple he has on his right cheek when he laughs and the way he would run his hand through his hair when we talked about hard topics like his dad passing. I miss his voice and getting to see his bare chest every night. *God, Emma, snap out of it; you're about to go on a date with someone else.*

I throw on a light pink matte lipstick and admire myself in the mirror. Maybe this date was a good idea because I can't even lie, I look good. This was the confidence boost I needed. My long brown hair is curled, and I have half of it up in a high pony and the rest of it falls over my shoulders. I went with a dark smokey look on my eyes and the exact right amount of pink on my cheeks that pair perfectly with my lips. My top is made of a thick material, so I decided against a bra, a brave choice for my C cups, which means my breasts are flowing over the top of my crop top and my nipples are poking through in a sexy but classy way. I know a lot of women with larger breasts cringe at the idea of going braless, but I love the feeling.

This may be the most effort I have put into myself in a long time. I look hot, like really hot, and when I leave the bathroom and head to the kitchen, my heart is pounding, waiting to see if and how Jay reacts. I try not to look at either my mother or Jay and head straight to the open wine bottle to pour myself a glass of my own because, despite my confidence, my hands are shaking. What if Jay doesn't even glance my way? What if he doesn't care one bit that I am going on a date? And even though Landon is not the guy I am interested in, this is still the first date I have been on since spring semester and I always get a tad nervous before a first date.

"Emma, honey, don't you look lovely. Where are you off to?" Loraine asks with the sweetest tone that has me wanting to burst out laughing but also slap her across the face. I guess her charade of playing a "loving mother" around Jay continues. I don't think she has ever given me a compliment in my whole life, and if Jay weren't here, I know she'd be making a comment about my curvy hips and how an outfit like this doesn't work on a body like mine. The last date I went on was with Dave in May, when I wore the lacy spaghetti strapped top that emphasized my breasts and tight jeans that made my butt look fantastic, but the minute she saw me, she said that with how I looked, my date would have no interest in me and I would be home in an hour. Dave, in fact, did not have those same thoughts. Not even close. He couldn't keep his hands off me all night, and I ended up staying over at his place. I will never forget how good it felt to see her surprised face when I walked in the next morning wearing what were clearly men's sweats. Ultimately, things didn't work out with him because he really had no drive or interest in his plans after college, which was not what I needed at the time. But boy did it feel good to prove her wrong.

Jay looks over at me after my mother's question, and before I can answer, I have to take a sip of wine to hide the smile that starts to form when I see the way he looks at me. His eyes look like they are about to pop out of his head as they roam all over my body, and his hand, that was about to be used to take a drink of his wine, is frozen in front of his face. Luckily, my mother's still staring at me and doesn't notice the way Jay is clearly ogling.

"I have a date," I say casually as I take another swig of wine.

"Oh, wonderful, who is he?" The game continues.

"A guy I met at the coffee shop."

"Where are you meeting him?" Jay chimes in, surprising me.

"Oh, he's picking me up here in a few minutes, and we're going to a bar," I say casually.

"Well, I'm off to take a bath. Have fun, sweetie," my mother says as she cheers her wine glass to the air and heads off to her room. The word sweetie on her lips sounds so strange and foreign that it shocks me a little. I don't respond; instead, I watch her as she walks away. She is unbelievable. That whole interaction was so fake. A part of me wishes that it was real, that this is how we always interact, and I hate myself for that. But that feeling is fleeting because I can feel Jay's eyes on me as I take another sip of wine and now that I'm alone with him, he is the only thing on my mind.

"You know it's better to meet somewhere on a first date? It's safer and easier to make a quick exit if you need to," he tells me, concern evident in his voice.

I don't show it, but on the inside, I am squealing. He's worried, and maybe even jealous. Or both. This is working. *Thank you, Jessica!*

"I'll be fine," I assure him.

"What do you know about the guy?" he continues.

"Uh, I know he likes coffee." I laugh, but Jay clearly does not think it's funny because he is still staring at me with an intensity that has me squeezing my thighs together.

"Give me your phone," he demands.

"What? Why?" I ask. His request takes me off guard.

"So I can put my number in it in case you need anything. You know I'll be up."

I hand him my phone willingly because the way he is staring at me has me eating out of the palm of his hand, and I'll do anything he asks me to. He puts his number in my phone and right as he hands it back to me, I get a text from Landon telling me he's out front.

"Well, that's my ride. Night, Jay."

"Please call me if you need anything," he repeats; a pleading look fills his eyes.

"I'll be fine, Jay," I reassure him and head to the door.

"Emma," he says, and I stop because the way my name flows off his tongue makes my legs want to give out. I can barely manage to turn around and face him with the trembling that is happening throughout my body.

"You really do look beautiful," he says and my heart may just flutter right out of my chest.

My mouth goes desert dry, and I barely manage a "thank you" before I turn and head outside to a date that I would really like to cancel right about now.

# CHAPTER 10

Even though it was nearly impossible to walk out of my house after Jay called me beautiful and even though I really am not interested in Landon, I'm surprisingly having a pretty good time. He's actually really funny and easy to talk to and honestly, I could see us becoming good friends. Not sure how he would feel about that and I definitely feel a little guilty for using him tonight, but he never has to know the truth.

After we finish a couple drinks, he asks if I want to go to his friend's party with him. College parties are not normally my idea of fun, but since I'm still scarred from the other night and have no desire to risk hearing Jay and Loraine having sex again, I agree. Besides, I really am having a good time with him and it feels good to give myself a break from studying and to feel like a normal college student for once.

The minute we walk into the party though, the entire mood of the night shifts, and I immediately regret agreeing to come here. Jay was right; I should have brought my own car. I take in my surroundings and am instantly reminded of the reason I do not do college parties. Not only do I not recognize a single person, which makes sense because Landon goes to a different college than I do, but we are in a large two-story house that is obviously shared by a bunch of boys whose mommies have clearly been picking up after them their entire lives. I'm not sure this house has ever been cleaned. Dirt and god knows what else crunch under my heels, every surface of furniture has a visible layer of dust on it and is topped with old beer cans and solo cups, and god, the *smell*. There are kegs in almost every corner, and the smell of cigarette smoke and marijuana stings the air. Don't get me wrong, I am not judging anyone for drinking or smoking, but how can anyone live like this? This house makes me want to go home and that is really saying something.

"You wanna drink?" Landon yells over the loud, awful music that booms through the house.

If I'm going to make it another minute in this house, I will definitely need a drink, and since I'm not the one driving, I agree to a drink and then head to find the bathroom. It takes me a couple minutes, but I find one upstairs, down a hallway. My phone chimes and when I shut the bathroom door behind me and check the screen, I can't contain the giddy feeling that knocks the air right out of my lungs. *"Don't hesitate to text if you need a ride,"* Jay's text reads.

My jaw aches at the ear-to-ear grin that covers my entire face. *Maybe I should have him come get me. I mean, I don't want to be here anyway.* I stare at my phone and contemplate it for a few more seconds before deciding against it for now. His text means he is still thinking about me. The plan is working. So, for now, I choose to ignore it and carry on with my night. At least for a little while longer in hopes it only makes him think about me more.

This is not my typical behavior with men. I am not my mother. I am confident and independent. I have never cared to make anyone jealous and I feel a little embarrassed about the way I am acting. But this whole situation is making me crazy. *He* is making me crazy. *I need that drink.*

When I find Landon, he hands me a lukewarm beer in a red solo cup, and I cringe, but down most of it in one sitting. The more I drink, the braver I become and the more likely I'll actually go through with asking Jay to come pick me up. Only once he has had a little more time to worry about me, of course. Because it's obvious that's what's happening. He is worried. About me. The thrill of that alone has more of an effect on me than the god-awful bud light in my hand.

Not even thirty minutes later, I'm in a corner talking to Landon and a wave of drowsiness hits me so hard I almost fall over. How many drinks have I had? Landon catches me around the waist, and I cling to him, so tired now I can barely stand.

"Hey, hey, you okay?" he whispers in my ear and moves his hands down, holding me up by the ass. I know in this second that something is very wrong. I manage enough strength to lift my head off his shoulder and look up at him.

Bile rises up my throat when I see the kind of look he's had in his eyes all night replaced with a terrifying hunger. Realization soars through me that he is not who I thought he was. That I am not his date anymore. I am his prey. I step back, away from him, and have to hold on to the wall to keep myself standing.

"No," I slur and hold up one hand, stopping him from coming any further. It doesn't work, though, because my muscles feel like jelly. He grabs my hand and pulls me back into him, grabbing my ass once again and pulling my body against his.

"NO," I try to speak louder, but the music is too loud, and there are too many people around to hear me. I start to panic now because he's guiding us to the downstairs hallway. From the outside looking in, it would probably just look as if Landon is taking care of his date that got too drunk. We pass a table that has a full cup of beer on it, and with every ounce of strength I have, I grab the cup and slam the whole thing in his face as hard as my frail muscles allow.

"What the fuck?" he hollers angrily, and I take this opportunity to pull myself up the stairs as fast as I can, adrenaline pumping through me and terror giving me the strength to make it up each step.

I make it to the bathroom I was in earlier and my hands are shaking as I slam the door and lock it. My body collapses onto the ground, all of that effort catching up to me. I can barely see straight, but somehow, I manage to grab my phone and click on the only name I can think of right now. The name at the top of my messages.

"Emma? Are you okay?" he answers frantically, clearly shocked that I am actually calling.

"No. I… I'm in a bathroom, I… I… I think someone… I think he put something in my… my drink." My words are slurring, and I pray he can understand at least some of what I'm saying.

"Emma, where are you?" he demands; fury clear in the tone of his voice.

"I… I don't know. Someone's house," I stammer.

"Emma, it's okay, but I need to know where you are, can you drop me your pin," he pleads.

Taking deep breaths, I focus on my phone screen and manage to drop my location to Jay right as a thud pounds on the door.

"Emma, come out of the bathroom," Landon's voice roars through the bathroom door.

"Go away," I cry.

"Who is that, Emma?" Jay asks.

"My date. Jay, I'm scared," I cry.

"I'm five minutes away. Where's the bathroom?" he asks calmly, trying to keep me calm as well, and I manage an "upstairs" right before I succumb to whatever it was that Landon put in my drink, and pass out.

I am awoken when someone starts slamming on the door, and I come to a little more when I hear Jay yelling my name. My arms are still so weak, but the sound of his voice gives me the strength to reach up and unlock the door. My arm immediately collapses back down to my side.

He throws the door open and is in front of me in less than a second. "Hey, hey, Emma, wake up, you need to stay awake, I'm getting you out of here." I can see him just barely through my blurred vision as he holds my face in his hands, looking into each of my eyes.

He picks me up off the ground and holds me in his arms as he walks us down the stairs. "Do you see him anywhere?" he whispers in my ear.

I try with everything in me to focus on all of the people, but I am so tired I can barely keep my eyelids open, so I shake my head no. Jay asks for his name and I manage to whisper "Landon."

"LANDON?" he yells, still holding me in his arms.

A girl who must have realized something serious is going on, says, "In the kitchen," and in a second, Jay is putting me down and asking the girl to help hold me up.

I start to panic when I know he has left me, but then I hear him from the kitchen. There is a very loud thud and a "What the fuck man?" from Landon, and I know Jay must have him pinned against a wall.

"How much did you give her?" Jay yells angrily.

"I don't know what you're talking about, man," Landon says through a nervous laugh, trying to play dumb.

There is a loud thud of flesh meeting flesh and with the gasps from the people around me, I can assume Jay laid one on him.

"How much?" Jay asks one more time with a tone that would have anyone trembling in fear.

"Just half a pill, man, but I didn't even touch her, I swear," Landon confesses.

Jay's hands are back on me in less than a second and I feel instant relief.

"I'd leave now; the cops will be on their way shortly!" he yells at the party.

"Come on, I'm taking you to the hospital," he tells me,

and I start to panic.

"No! You can't." I can't afford hospital bills. That would derail everything.

"Emma, you've been drugged. We need to get you checked up, and if you want to press charges, you will probably need a blood test."

He's right; I know he is. But at this moment, none of that matters. Spending any more time in my house with Loraine than I have planned sounds worse to me than not being able to press charges. It's a dumb decision, but years of emotional abuse at the hands of your own mother will make you do crazy things.

"Jay, no. No hospitals, *please*. You're a vet. Surely you can help," I plead, but I have no idea if the desperation got through to him because before he could answer, I passed out again.

# CHAPTER 11

Terror strikes through me as I roll over in a bed that is definitely not my own. I shoot up and then immediately have to put my hands down on the bed to stabilize myself as a wave of dizziness hits me. There is a clock on the nightstand that reads four a.m. and I can barely make out the rest of the room with the help of the moon shining through the window.

I am in a large room, furnished with only this bed, two nightstands, and a dresser. I notice a small-looking medical device on one of the nightstands. I look down to find that I am not in my clothes from the night before and instead am in a large t-shirt and boxer shorts. Some blurry memories from the night before flash through my head and I cringe when I remember Jay carrying me out of that awful party. I cringe again when I think about how stupid I was to put myself in that position. Jay was right, and I'm disappointed in myself for putting my pride before my safety.

Jay. So, that is where I'm at? Did he change me? My cheeks flush at the thought. He is not in the bed with me, not that he would be because he is dating my mother, so I assume this is a guest room. Or he's on the couch. I still can't believe how protective of me he was last night. But is that because he feels for me in a romantic way or a fatherly way? I wince at that thought, but it could very well be the truth. He is with my *mother*, after all. If they got married, he would be my stepdad. My eyes shut tightly at that image, immediately trying to push it out of my mind.

He didn't take me home, though. He brought me back to his place, which means he did not want to explain any of this to Loraine. That has to mean something, right?

Realizing my mouth is as dry as cotton, I get out of bed and try to find the kitchen. Which is not hard because it doesn't take me long to work out that I'm in an apartment and the kitchen is a small hallway away from the bedroom I was just in. Jay isn't in the kitchen or living room and for a second, I wonder if he went back to my house, and the thought majorly bums me out. Would he rather dump me here alone than spend a night away from Loraine?

Not knowing where he keeps his cups, I start quietly opening cabinets until I find them. I take one, head to the fridge, and stick it under the waterspout. My cup is about halfway full when I hear Jay's groggy voice behind me.

"How are you feeling?"

His question fills the silent kitchen and I yelp, dropping the water-filled cup all over his kitchen floor. Even though it startled me, it's impossible not to notice how sexy his sleepy voice is.

"Shit. I'm sorry," I say as I grab a random towel and drop to the floor to clean up the mess I made. I can sense him walking toward me, and when he drops to the ground in front of me, our faces are only mere inches apart. I keep my eyes on the water I'm trying to wipe up, but I'm very aware that he is in nothing but a pair of sweatpants.

He grabs my hands, stopping me from the cleaning I'm doing. "Emma. Please stop and look at me."

I try to keep my hands from shaking at his touch because this most definitely does not feel like a protective fatherly moment. Our eyes meet, and I can see the genuine concern and worry etched on his face.

"I'm fine," I say, but as more memories from last night start to come back, I remember how terrifying it was, and Jay must be able to see the lingering fear all over my face.

"Come here," he says gently as he sits on the floor and pulls me into him.

He has me in his lap in seconds, and my body reacts immediately to being engulfed in his arms. There is no way he can't feel the goosebumps covering my skin and my heart that's beating out of my chest a mile a minute. His skin touching mine makes my body come alive in a way I've never felt before, and I don't ever want this moment to end. I'm envious that my mother gets to feel this every night. Does she appreciate it or is she too drunk to even realize how good this feels? All I know is, she doesn't deserve it.

"I'm so sorry, Emma. I want to kill that piece of shit so bad, I don't think I've ever been so angry," he confesses, his muscles clenched underneath me. I can feel the anger radiating through him as he holds me.

More memories of the night start flooding back. I remember how Landon would not let me go. I remember the fear I felt when I realized he was leading us to a room. I remember how physically hard it was to throw the drink in his face and get up the stairs, and I realize now that my whole body is shaking. Jay pulls me in tighter, my body folding perfectly inside his. He holds me like this for a while until eventually the trauma from last night combined with the feeling of being held by Jay overcomes me. I sob in his arms. He pulls me tighter into him, and my body responds on its own, adjusting so that my legs now straddle his. . I don't think about how this position is undoubtedly a very bad idea, instead I bury my head in his neck and let the tears come. Every emotion from these last few weeks comes boiling to the surface, and I can't hold it in any longer. It's all too much. I sob, my tears covering his skin.

Minutes go by and with the feel of Jay's hand rubbing up and down my back, I start to calm down a bit. My breathing starts to steady, and I'm able to take a long, deep breath as my body relaxes. My head is still buried in-between his neck and shoulder, but once Jay feels the tension in my body start to ease, he wraps his arms tighter around my body and lets out his own deep breath he must have been holding.

"I've missed you," he whispers in my ear. A shiver falls down my spine at the implication of his words and the way his breath felt on my skin as he spoke them.

I'm unsure how to respond to him. I want him to elaborate more, but now that I'm not crying, all I can think about is the position we're in; my forehead lying on his bare shoulder, my legs wrapped around his waist, his arms wrapped around me, holding me close to him. And then I feel him under me. The bulge in his shorts starts to harden under the pressure of my body. He doesn't say a word, but

I can feel his heartbeat pounding right along with mine. I am not sure what to do. I mean, I know what I should do. I should get up and go back to the room I was in and stop this moment with my mother's boyfriend before it goes any further. But I can't bring myself to do that. Not while I'm here on top of him, his dick hard under my groin. Not while it is *me* that is making him aroused like this. Which can only mean one thing. I have the same effect on him that he has on me. So instead of getting up, instead of going back to that room like I should, I grind my hips slowly down against him, his length stiffening even more with the impact.

Neither of us makes a sound; the only noise in the whole apartment is our heavy breathing. His hands move to my waist and his grip on me tightens, urging me to push into him again, so I do. A pool of moisture appears between my thighs, and a throb forms so intense that if I moved the right way, I know I would climax right on top of him.

His erection is in full force now and is pushing hard against me. There is nothing but a couple of thin layers of fabric between us, and I think I may pass out. Jay's hands are still gripping tightly on my waist, holding me in place, his head buried in my neck, breathing heavily into my ear. My nails are digging into his bare skin on his back, and just as I am about to push myself down onto him again to relieve the ache both of us are feeling right now, he breaks the moment.

"Emma." He groans, and even though his voice is so sexy that it makes my slit grow even more wet, I can tell he is ending this moment before it can go any further.

"You should go back to bed," he speaks again; his tone is more final now.

I don't want to, but the finality in his voice snaps me back to our awful reality and I nod my head, climb off his lap, and head back to the room without a look back. I climb back into the bed, but there is no way I can sleep now. My hand moves down, and my fingers make contact with my folds. I don't think I've ever been this wet or turned on before in my entire life. My fingers don't hesitate or wait one second, and after making only three circles around my nub, I climax. I don't cover my mouth or stifle my cries, though, because I want him to hear me. I want him to feel just as tortured as I did when he made me get off of him and come back to this room.

My breath is staggered, and when I think back to the position Jay and I were just in, I can feel myself getting aroused again. My fingers weren't enough. Jay is the only one who could get rid of this need inside me, and he sent me away. I roll over to find my phone sitting on the nightstand and turn it on because I am way too frustrated to sleep now. A text pops up from two hours ago, and it's from Jay. *"If you wake up scared, I'm just down the hall. You're safe now."*

My heart clenches in my chest, despite the anger I just felt toward him. Whatever is going on between us is not one-sided and I know that with one hundred percent certainty now.

# CHAPTER 12

The next morning, Jay helped me make a statement to the police, although they said without any evidence it would be hard to make a charge, and then he dropped me off at campus in one of his T-shirts and my jeans I wore the night before. There was no discussion of our moment in the kitchen, and neither of us attempted to bring it up. But I was thankful to have him with me when I made the statement.

It has been a week since then. The following night, I heard them both in my mother's room having what sounded like a serious discussion, and it even sounded like my mother was crying. I tried to eavesdrop, but they were so quiet all that I could hear were muffled voices and noises.

A part of me thought for sure Jay was breaking up with her. There is no way he would stay with her after what happened with us at his place, right? I stayed up all night that night, heart pounding, waiting for him to leave or maybe even knock on my door, but nothing. Eventually, the voices stopped, and his truck was still there when I left early the next morning. I was devastated.

Every day, I open his name on my phone and debate texting. Debate telling him how awful she is and I hate that they're still together. How much I hate him right now for putting me through this. But I always stop myself, unable to actually go through with it because I don't hate him. I can't hate him even when I try to. After that night at his apartment, I think I'm even more in love with him than before.

Neither he nor my mother are in the living room when I walk inside the house Friday night after my shift. I sigh and debate leaving because my heart can't bear hearing them together again. But I'm exhausted, and all I want to do is eat and go to bed. I have been working and studying at Snaps since my last class ended before noon. My stomach growling is the only noise I can hear in this entire house. I rummage through the pantry and fridge to see what, if any, groceries we have. I didn't want to spend money, but looking at the minimal options, I wish I had stopped somewhere on the way home.

I grab some bread and cheese and settle on a grilled cheese sandwich — fast and easy. And also the only real option. I make it and scarf it down in probably less than ten minutes. At the sink, as I scrub my knife and plate, my mind wanders to Jay. Since he's been coming around, I hardly ever have to do dishes anymore. The sink is always empty and squeaky clean when I get home at night, and since I know it is definitely not Loraine's doing, that only leaves Jay.

"SHIT!" I yell, throwing the knife I used to cut my sandwich down in the sink. In my trance of imagining Jay here shirtless, cleaning dishes, I stopped paying attention and instead of bringing the sponge back down over the knife, it was the outside of my thumb that ran over the ridges. The ferocity with which I was scrubbing gave the serrated knife the opportunity to slice open my skin. I hold my hand under the running water when Jay emerges in the kitchen, quickly running up behind me. His hand immediately comes to my lower back as he tries to inspect my hand. My body flinches away from his touch, all of the anger I have pent up towards him making my body react before my brain can.

"Emma..." he pleads as he grabs my hand and pulls it up to his face so he can see the wound. He puts it back under the water to let more blood rinse off, and I wince. He pulls it back into the light to look at it again.

"It won't need stitches, but it's a good cut. Do you have any first-aid stuff here?" he asks, and I nod. I lead him back to my bathroom, and when he shuts the door behind us, my stomach twists into knots.

He cleans the wound with some hydrogen peroxide and then rubs some Neosporin over it with a Q-tip. His hands are gentle and careful, and I imagine how good he must be at his job. He puts a large Band-Aid on it and then wraps it in bandage wrap. When he is finished, I expect him to get up. Or to say something. But he doesn't. He doesn't move at all; his hands are still holding on to my injured one. I look up at him at the same time that he looks up to me, and our eyes lock. My heart rate quickens. My breath catches. I'm afraid to move. To do anything that could break this moment. He brings his forehead down to mine and my eyes close at the contact. I'm not sure how long we stay like that. It may have only been ten seconds, but it feels like an eternity.

Eventually, without a word, Jay pulls away, walks out of the bathroom, and goes back to Loraine's room, shattering my heart and soul into a million pieces.

Another week goes by without seeing him. Another week without hearing his voice. But he is all I can think about. He takes up all the space in my brain, making it extremely difficult to focus on the one thing I should be. College. Studying. Graduation. It has all taken a back seat to Jay. One second later, I'm angry at him. One second, I miss him. And then the next second, I'm turned on, daydreaming about how his dick felt under me while I straddled him in his kitchen.

It feels as if I am on the wooden roller coaster at the theme park that bounces you around until your head hurts and you want to vomit. I have only been on a ride like that once when my middle school got gifted a field trip to Six Flags in San Antonio. We got charter buses and left before the sun came up and got back after it went down. There were a couple of other schools that got to go too and I met a nice girl that also seemed to not have any friends. We hung out all day, riding all of the rides together. It is one of the happiest days from my childhood. And it was spent with a stranger. We both *hated* the wooden roller coaster. We had to sit for thirty minutes afterward to get the nausea, dizziness, and pounding headache to go away. That is how I feel after an interaction with Jay.

It kills me not knowing what he's thinking. I knew he felt what I was feeling as we held each other at his place and when he fixed up my cut finger. The fact that we have had those moments and he is still with my mother is driving me absolutely insane. Even growing up with an emotionally abusive mother, my emotions were never this up and down. The moments we have shared have been so intense, so *real*, that I refuse to believe I am the only one affected by them. I know he feels our connection, so why is he still with her? What has she said to him to make him feel the need to stay? This thought has kept me up every night for the past week.

# CHAPTER 13

Fall semester is flying by. Halloween has already come and gone. Which I spent at work and then at the library. Jessica tried to get me to go to a Halloween party with her, but with how much I have put school on the back burner lately, and with how awful the last college party was that I went to, I decided against it. And now it's already November. Finals will be here before I know it, and it is only a matter of time before I'm able to get a job and get my own place. It's been hard to juggle school and work on top of this mess with Jay, but since I haven't seen him much recently, I have been able to get my focus somewhat back on track.

"So, no new updates with Mr. Asshole?" Jessica asks the minute she shows up for our Friday afternoon shift. The thing I love most about being friends with Jessica is that she will be on your side and have your back always.

"Nope. We have both successfully avoided the hell out of each other ever since the knife incident," I say and rub my finger over the small pink line that now sits on my thumb. It healed rather quickly after Jay worked his magic, but I'll have a small reminder of him on my thumb forever now.

"Man, I was hoping for some more drama!" She teases and then adds in a more serious tone, "Although I don't ever want you going to any more parties unless I'm with you, okay?"

"Okay," I agree.

Jessica was distraught after I told her what happened with Landon. She blamed herself even when I told her a hundred times not to because it was absolutely not her fault. But since she was the one that encouraged me to go on the date, she felt as if it were her fault, despite my constant assurance that the only one at fault was Landon.

"I still can't believe they just let Landon off. It seems like men can do anything they want with no repercussions," Jessica says as she starts cleaning the espresso machine very aggressively.

"There wasn't enough evidence for them to even charge him with anything. Which is probably my fault because I didn't go to the hospital and get a blood test," I reminded her.

"That is such bullshit; your word should be enough. If he ever shows his face here again, I will kill him."

Her loyalty and threat to murder makes me smile, and I stop what I'm doing and hug her. She squeezes me back as tight as possible, and my heart warms. I will truly miss working with her, but I know now more than ever that our friendship has blossomed beyond just coworkers.

I want to bring us out of this depressing conversation, so I change the subject. "I'm so close! Less than two months till graduation. I can do it. And then I won't have to see either of them again," I say to her, even though the idea of never seeing Jay again leaves a pit in my stomach.

"I still can't believe you felt his actual dick. Like you

straddled your mom's boyfriend and felt his actual penis!" she whispers, but not quietly enough, and the middle-aged woman behind the register stares at us like we are crazy.

"She's kidding!" I say as I force a smile and take her order. "She's writing a book!" I add, trying to play this off as something funny and not what it actually is – terribly awful and humiliating. She doesn't say a word other than "I'll take a vanilla latte with a pump of hazelnut" and then glares at us as she walks off.

"I mean, good GOD, Jessica!" I exclaim.

"Oh my god, she came out of nowhere!" Jessica says, cracking up at the awkward situation. I shake my head at my crazy friend but can't help but laugh as well.

"Well?" she asks, not wanting to drop the conversation.

"Well, what?" I question.

"Did it feel big?" Thankfully, she actually whispers this time.

"I'm not answering that," I state.

"Come on! Give me some juicy deets, please!"

Rolling my eyes, I give her what she wants: "Fine, yes, it felt huge," I admit. And it did. To be honest, I haven't been able to stop thinking about it ever since. Even between two layers of clothing, I could feel how big he was and I've thought about it every night since.     Even right now at work, in the middle of this conversation with Jessica, I find myself lost in desire. But Jessica's response snaps me back to reality.

"AHHH yes! Maybe one day you and your mom will be Eskimo sisters." She laughs but then stops abruptly, realizing she took it too far.

"Shit, Emma, sorry, that was probably too far." She quickly apologizes.

I am gaping at her when I say, "Uh, you think?" But after a few seconds, we both burst out laughing. I mean, it is not at all funny, of course. But really, what else can I do in this crazy situation? And honestly, nothing will make you less horny than the thought of you and your mom as Eskimo sisters. And on top of that, it really did feel good to just laugh with my friend.

# Chapter 14

When I pull up to the house after my afternoon shift, it is nearly six o'clock, and Jay's truck is already in the driveway. For a second, I contemplate just leaving and going somewhere else, but I forgot my laptop charger here this morning. So even if I want to go to the library or back to Snaps to study, I need to go in and get that. I sigh. I guess avoiding Jay ends tonight.

I decide to keep my head down and go straight to my room, change out of my work clothes, grab my charger, and go back to Snaps for a fun Friday night study session. Honestly, it sounds way better than spending the rest of the night hiding in my room. Because that is my only option if I stay here. No way in hell would I hang out in the living room with the two of them.

When I open the front door and walk into my house, I see my mother sprawled on the couch and a bottle of vodka sitting on the coffee table. Jay is standing in front of the TV with his arms crossed as he stares down at Loraine, a scowl on his face so intense that it even makes me a little nervous.

There is an obvious tension between the two of them that is hard to ignore, and every part of me wants to know what's going on, but I have to remind myself that this is not my relationship and, therefore, not my problem.

When Jay looks up at me, the scowl on his face softens just a bit. I clench my jaw and give him a small nod, but then do as I said I was going to; keep my head down and go straight to my room to gather my things and get the hell out. But as I walk past them to try and get to the hallway, my mother's voice stops me in my tracks.

"Why don't you just take Emma if you really neeeeed someone to go with you."

My eyes close and I let out a sigh as I realize my plan of getting in and out may not work out after all. I open my eyes and debate ignoring her. I could just pretend they aren't here. Better yet, I could pretend they don't exist. Walk right into my room and leave. But every cell in my body is fighting against what I *could* do. What I *should* do. Because if I am being completely honest, the idea of going somewhere with Jay, of spending time with him outside of this house, outside of the confines of Loraine, is something I know I won't refuse.

"Go where?" I ask as calmly as I can, not letting any ounce of emotion show on my face.

"A banquet, but it's fine. Emma, I know it's a Friday night; this is not your problem," he tells me.

I look at my mother, who is clearly drunk and who is clearly the one supposed to be going with him, and I am so tired of her bullshit that I ask her flat out, "And why can't you go?" even though I already know the answer. I just want her to have to say the words out loud.

"She's drunk," Jay answers before my mother can even get a word out.

My mother and I snort at the same time. Me because,

of course, she is. I'm not the least bit surprised. But at least she's finally showing her true colors to Jay. My mother snorts because she's drunk and probably knows she messed up but is putting up a front like it's not a big deal.

"Nice, Loraine," I tell her. My eyes meet hers, and I don't back down until she looks away.

"Well, I just didn't know it was such a big deal," she slurs.

It's Jay's turn to snort now. He is pissed. But this moment doesn't feel as good as I thought it would. I only feel bad for him. But I am not sure his girlfriend's daughter, whom he has had multiple intimate moments with, should accompany him to his work event. Even if said girlfriend's daughter really wants to go.

"Why can't you go alone?" I ask him.

"I signed us both up to help with the dinner buffet. That starts at seven," he says as he looks at his watch and nervously taps his foot on the ground. "They're counting on us, and there will be multiple veterinarians, technicians, and shelter employees from the area there. It's an important event." He runs his hand through his hair in frustration.

I don't want it to, but every ounce of anger I have felt toward him the past couple weeks vanishes completely. My heart betrays me, and it hurts for him even though it shouldn't.

"Is it formal?" I ask.

"I'd say you could borrow a dress, but with your hips, I doubt you'd fit into anything of mine," Loraine chimes in from the couch.

I see the shocked look Jay gives her at this comment, and for the first time in my entire life, I am thankful for an offensive remark from Loraine. Thankful that Jay is finally starting to see her for who she really is.

"Jesus, Loraine, what the hell!" he says to her, disgust on his face, and my mother is too drunk to even realize what she's done. I'm surprised she is even still conscious, with how empty that bottle is. She manages to stand up and stumble past us to her room, not looking at either of us as she passes.

"It's fine, Jay. Is it formal?" I ask again once she is out of the room; my skin is too thick at this point to feel the sting from a comment like that.

"Yes, it's formal," he answers and gives me an apologetic look. He opens and closes his mouth multiple times as if he wants to say something else, but he seems to be struggling to get the words out.

"Okay, give me twenty minutes," I say, saving him from having to apologize for Loraine or whatever it was that he couldn't get out.

Despite the fact that I know this is a terrible idea because it will only make things more complicated and I know my heart will only be more broken after tonight, I can't help the excitement that bubbles up as I turn to head to my room to get ready.

I decide on a form-fitting black velvet dress that I wore to a sports banquet I went to last year with a guy I was seeing for a couple of weeks. It's the only long, formal dress that I own. It's floor length, but has a slit that starts at my upper right thigh, making it sexy but not scandalous.

It has thin straps that rest on my shoulders and allows for just the tiniest bit of cleavage. I'm sure it isn't as nice as something Loraine has in her closet, but it'll have to do. I slick my hair back up into a neat, high pony. Touch up my makeup and throw on some simple dangle earrings. Then I grab my nicest black heels from my closet and am ready to go in fifteen minutes.

As I stare at myself in my full-length mirror that hangs behind my bedroom door, I find it hard not to judge myself right now. *What the hell are you doing, Emma?* My feelings for Jay are getting harder to control, and I'm supposed to only be worrying about graduating and starting my new life, but I have somehow fallen completely off course and am now stuck in an extremely weird love triangle with my mother and her boyfriend.

"Just this one night. You'll go to this banquet because it's a nice thing to do, but after this, you're done with your mother and Jay for good," I tell myself in the mirror before I open the door and head out to a very different evening I planned on having just twenty minutes ago.

Right before I'm about to walk out of the hallway and enter the living room, where I can see Jay sitting on the couch, waiting, I hear my mother's bedroom door open behind me. I can feel her presence, and I wait for the blow that I know is coming. But before she can open her mouth, I turn to face her, to will her into saying something hurtful to me in front of Jay.

Our eyes meet, and I can tell immediately when she sees me in my dress how sour she is that I actually am going to the banquet with Jay, despite her being the one that suggested it.

"Are you happy with yourself right now, Mother?" I ask her before she can even get a word in.

She looks me up and down before she responds, "I wouldn't bend over too much in that dress, don't want to bust any zippers." And with that, she turns around and walks back into her bedroom, shutting the door behind her.

I let out a sigh, trying hard to let her second insult of the night bounce off my skin. I turn around and head to the living room, where I see Jay at the end of the hall staring at me, his mouth tight and his hands clenched at his sides. I can tell right away that he heard that whole interaction. I find it hard to meet his eyes as I walk past him, out the front door, and straight to the passenger door of his truck. He follows slowly behind, and comes to my side to open the door for me. I can't look at him. As much as I wanted him to hear Loraine say those awful things, I find it hard not to feel embarrassed at my body being insulted twice in front of him tonight. I feel self-conscious in this dress now, my normal confidence faltering at Loraine's words. I feel sexy in this dress. I *know* that I look sexy. But when your mother makes fun of your appearance, it doesn't matter how thick your skin is; those words will eventually seep right through.

Carefully, so I don't bust any zippers, I climb into the seat and Jay closes the door behind me. He walks around to the driver's seat and climbs in to sit next to me. My eyes are glued ahead, focused on a stain on the garage door that has been there since I can remember, but I can feel Jay's eyes on me, burning my skin and making my hands tremble in my lap.

Slowly, he turns his body towards mine and leans over the middle console to reach me. His hand settles on my thigh, right at the top of the slit where my dress meets my skin. I can see the goosebumps that cover my skin at the contact, and I wonder if he notices them too.

"Look at me, Emma," he whispers, and I can't. I don't want to cry in front of him. I don't want to ruin my makeup because of a stupid comment that Loraine made that shouldn't even be affecting me this much.

"Emma, please look at me," he repeats and then uses his other hand to grab my chin and guide my eyes to meet his.

"You look fucking incredible," he tells me. His eyes stare straight into mine, and it feels as if they are reaching into my soul. Healing me from all the wounds Loraine has caused me.

I let out a noise that could be both a laugh and a cry, and honestly, I'm unsure as to which it is. Maybe both. I break our eye contact to shake away the tears that start to form at his compliment.

"Hey," he says as he grabs my chin again and pulls my face back up to meet his. "Is that how it always is?" he asks with a worried look on his face as he nods back at the house.

I don't have the energy to lie anymore, nor do I want to, but I feel drained, so a simple "yes" is the only thing I can manage.

He shakes his head and pulls my face closer to his so he can rest his forehead on mine. We only stay this way for a few seconds, but it's enough time to pull my heart strings even closer to his.

He pulls away from me and starts the car, and I have to wrap my arms around myself to control the trembling that has erupted throughout my body from just that brief interaction. *How am I gonna make it through this whole night?*

# Chapter 15

When we get to the event, it's clear that this night is actually a pretty big deal. The venue is very formal; there are probably a hundred people here at least, and the space is filled with fancy tables covered in dark blue silky tablecloths and elegant centerpieces. The whole right wall of the space has auction tables set up in front of it.

Jay told me they were raising money for the local animal shelters around the Houston area. This was clearly something that had been planned for a long time, and although I can easily believe that my mother got drunk, not only knowing the importance of this event but also how important it was to Jay, I am no less furious at her. But then again, she probably doesn't know what is important to Jay. It's obvious to me now that she doesn't know him like I do. She is finally letting her true colors show, and I don't feel one ounce of guilt at the relief I feel at that.

We put our stuff down in our seats, although my spot at the table has a 'Loraine' name tag on it. I grimace and flip it over quickly, not even caring if Jay notices. I am done pretending anything when it comes to Loraine. But if he does notice, he doesn't say anything.

We head away from the table so Jay can show me to the buffet we'll be helping serve. There are caterers walking around passing out appetizers and bartenders making drinks, so I'm a little surprised that as guests, we're serving the buffet. Not that I mind whatsoever. Jay must have noticed my observation and answered the question I had been thinking to myself.

"All the veterinarians decided we'd help serve and work at the event to show our support to our staff and all the other members of Houston that help take care of our animals. We are only signed up for a thirty-minute shift, so we don't have to do this for too long." He winks at me with a smile that has me grabbing onto the table so I don't melt straight into the ground.

"I don't mind at all," I reassure him.

If I'm honest with myself, I'm a little more than excited to be here right now with Jay. *Too* excited. And I know that I shouldn't be. Especially after everything that has happened between us. But I am. I can't help it, and I silently thank whatever gods are above us for the vodka that made its way down Loraine's throat today.

Our thirty-minute shift ends quickly, and then it's our turn to grab some of the mushroom chicken, lobster mac and cheese, and roasted asparagus. My mouth waters as we make our way back to our table and take our seats. Jay introduces me to his colleagues and other veterinarians that are sitting at the table with us as "his friend Emma," and truthfully, I don't mind that title. "Friend" is the preferred option for what he could actually introduce me as.

Soon after we eat, the auction starts. By this point, I have had a couple glasses of wine and am feeling way more relaxed and comfortable than I was at the start of the night. Jay seems to feel this way too because he is cracking jokes with me, whispering gossip in my ear that he knows about some of the guests. Each time his breath makes contact with my neck, goosebumps shield my skin. As if covering me with an armor that will hopefully protect myself from what's to come. I hope it works 'cause with how I am feeling right now with his lips so close to my face, I know I'm in for a world of trouble.

We talk and giggle and for a brief moment, I let myself imagine that this is real. Because even though I know it isn't, in this moment right now, it feels like it is. It feels *real*. Especially when Jay puts his hand on my thigh and leans in close. "You look beautiful, Emma. You always do. And anyone who doesn't see that is crazy."

My hands tremble in my lap for thirty minutes afterward as I try to bring my heart rate back down to normal.

There are lots of auction items, including some gorgeous paintings of various animals, really nice dog crates, beds, and other pet supplies. There are also some big items, like dinners at fancy steakhouses in Houston and even a travel package to a beach house in Florida.

As soon as the bidding begins, I notice Jay constantly checking his phone. He checks it and almost immediately puts it back in his pocket, only sometimes will he text back and respond to whoever is blowing up his phone.

My mind automatically jumps to Loraine. Maybe she feels guilty. Maybe she is on her way here right now. I feel as if the walls are closing in around me as I think about how humiliating it would be to have to go home when

Jay's real date shows up.

I try to push the thought out of my head. It could be *anyone*. But it could also be Loraine. Of course, it could be her. Regardless of the events that led me to be here tonight, it is she who gets to call herself Jay's. Not me.

Frozen to my seat, I watch in horror as the bet Jay placed on a nice steakhouse dinner gets picked. I feel sick at the image of him and Loraine sitting in a fancy restaurant together.

My body tenses, and I can't look at him anymore. I don't want to be here any longer, and I definitely don't want to see him win a night out with my mother. I get up quickly and race to the bathroom, stopping at the bar first to grab another wine. I down half of it by the time I get to the bathroom. I set it on the sink counter and grab the counter with both hands to steady myself, breathing deep breaths in and out to try and push these feelings out of me. And also, to try and sober up, as I realize I'm quite drunk after the *multiple* glasses of Malbec. I let my head fall because I'm too embarrassed to even look at the person staring back at me in the mirror. Eventually, after a few long, deep breaths, I pick up my head to give myself a good, long look. Who is she? I don't know this girl staring back at me anymore. Jay has completely altered my entire universe, and I am angry at myself for letting him have such an effect on me.

I have become so focused on my relationship with Jay, my mother's boyfriend, that I have forgotten what matters most right now. My college education. Graduation is in just a couple of months. Getting my own place and distancing myself from Loraine is what I'm supposed to be focusing on. Instead, I have entangled myself in her love life. Not only that, but I have fallen in love with her boyfriend. And even as I stare at myself and try to remember everything that should matter to me most, my mind can only focus on Jay. How it felt when he grabbed my thigh and told me how gorgeous I looked. How his breath felt on my skin as he whispered into my ear at the table. The sound of his laugh and how sexy his smile is. It engulfs every thought I have.

I want more than anything to have the strength to walk out of here, grab a cab, and leave him alone to sit at the table and text Loraine, but I can't. I can't walk away from him. I am too invested now. But I want to make him feel like I do. I want to hurt him like I'm hurting. Most importantly, I want to make him forget about my mother.

Chugging the rest of my wine, I give myself another hard, long look and walk out of the bathroom to do the one thing I know will grab his attention, because it's worked before.

By the time I leave the bathroom, the auction is over, and the dancing has started. The band that was playing quietly in the background this whole time is now booming through the venue and has become the center of the banquet. People have cleared their tables for the most part and are either slow dancing on the dance floor, hanging next to the bar, or checking out the auction items they won.

Going to the bar to get yet another glass of wine, I keep my eyes peeled for two things; Jay and any other man that lingers on me for a long enough period of time that shows me he's interested.

Before I can even order my drink, my eyes land on a man across the room that is clearly checking me out, his eyes blatantly scanning over my body and then dawdling at my breasts. I let my eyes linger back to his, giving him a sweet, but sexy, soft smile. It takes about two seconds for him to start making his way over here.

*Gotcha.*

My eyes still wander around as I wait for him to make his way over to me, looking all over for Jay. But there is no sign of him. My mind immediately drifts to the worst-case scenarios. Is he on the phone with Loraine? Or God, even worse, did he leave to be with her? I don't think he would do that, but what do I know really? Before I have time to dwell on it any longer, the man from across the room has made his way over to me.

"Hello," he says to me as he reaches his hand out for me to shake. "I'm Randall, I don't think I've seen you around before. Are you a vet?" he asks.

I take his hand and give it a good shake as I answer, "No, I'm just here with a friend, my name is Emma." I tell him in a way that makes it seem like I'm available and interested, even though I am not. But I'm good at this. Whether my mother wants to believe it or not, I know how to talk to a man.

"Well, Emma, I'm glad you're here tonight, and if you don't mind me saying, you look amazing," he compliments.

"Thank you, Randall, you look pretty good yourself." He is tall, but not as tall as Jay, although he is bulkier than him. Jay is lean and toned, while Randall's muscles are huge. The muscle man has never been my type, but his buzz cut paired with his navy-blue suit suits him, and I can't deny he is quite attractive.

"Would you like to dance?" he asks as he points to the dance floor, where another slow song has just started.

"Sure," I tell him as I set my wine down and take the hand he's holding out for me.

I realize pretty quickly that I really don't care to slow dance with him. Or to be talking with him at all. But I want to see Jay's reaction. And by this point, I'm four glasses of wine down, so I take his hand and follow him to join the crowd of people moving together on the dance floor.

Randall leads us in the dance, with one hand holding mine and the other low on my back. The touch of him on my skin does absolutely nothing. My heart rate stays normal, my breath stays steady, and not one goosebump erupts on my skin. He is funny, though; I will give him that. It gives him a charm that makes being in his company undeniably enjoyable.

I'm mid-laugh when I see him. Jay is staring at us from across the room. No, he is *glaring* at us from across the room. The look in his eyes sends a thrill through me, and it's impossible to notice that his eyes on me from a hundred feet away have more of an effect on my body than Randall's hand that is currently on my back.

*There you are*, I think to myself as I continue letting Randall's hand rest on my lower back. My plan is working. I can tell just by the look on Jay's face.

I stare back at him, laughing once again at one of

Randall's jokes, and this only makes Jay's face harden even more, but I don't take my eyes off him.

Jay quickly makes his way over to us, and even though I can tell he's angry, and even though I am angry at him myself, my pulse quickens, anxious for him to close the gap between us.

He walks right up to us. Coming in so close, it's impossible to keep dancing. Both Randall and I stop at the presence of Jay's body breaking us apart.

"Jay, good to see you, man!" Randall says as he claps Jay on the back, unaware of the weird situation I've put him in.

Jay doesn't take his eyes off me as he responds, "Nice to see you, Randall. I'm going to cut in if you don't mind."

Wow, they actually know each other; this worked out better than I thought.

"Uh, sure…" Randall says, looking between the both of us, confused. "If that's okay with Emma?" he adds, now that he has clearly picked up on the uncomfortable situation. He really is a gentleman, and I feel a little guilty about using him. But not so guilty that I regret it.

"Yah, thanks, Randall; it was really nice to meet you," I tell him, knowing he has served his purpose flawlessly.

Jay is still clearly fuming, but grabs me and pulls me into him to continue the dance since a new slow song has started. He grabs my hand tightly and pulls my body close to his. His hand now rests on my lower back, right where Randall's had, but this time my body comes to life at the contact. Each time I feel his thumb rub over my dress, an electric current shoots through my entire body, straight to my core. It takes everything in me to remain calm. To remember that I am angry with him, and if I bring my lips to his right now, like my body clearly wants to, it would do no good.

We are dancing way more intimately than I had with Randall – way more intimately than a man and his girlfriend's daughter should be dancing. Our bodies meld together as if one. He doesn't say one word as he guides us to the song, and this only pisses me off. What is this game he's playing with me? How dare he get mad I dance with someone else while he has clearly been texting Loraine for the last hour. While I have had to listen as he fucked her.

"Seriously, Jay, you didn't have to be so rude to Randall; we were just dancing," I tell him sharply.

"Yah and you're here with me, Emma; did you forget that?" he says through gritted teeth.

Is he serious? His comment is enough to break the trance his touch has on me, and I push him away.

"Are you kidding me?" I whisper, but I'm angry now, and it's taking everything in me not to make a scene.

"It was my mother who was supposed to be your date tonight, not me. Or don't you remember? Actually, how could you possibly forget? You've been texting her all night. And I know y'all fuck; I've had to listen to the two of you for god's sake, so if anyone needs to remember anything tonight, it's you, not me," I proclaim a little louder this time.

His face goes pale, and for a second, he's speechless. I'm a little embarrassed at the scene I'm starting to make, but the wine has taken over.

"When?" he asks, barely louder than a breath.

"A couple weeks ago," I answer, and he shuts his eyes and shakes his head as if he were trying to make all of this stop.

"Emma, we should go," he whispers and grabs my arm to pull me off the dance floor.

"Let go!" I yell as I yank my arm away. Jay lets me go easily because the few people near us turn to look our way, and I know right away that it's time to leave. I'm drunk and mad at him, but I don't want to ruin the night for other people. I walk quickly over to our table, grab my bag, and turn around to storm past Jay.

He is behind me in a matter of minutes, yelling my name as I fly through the parking lot to his truck.

"Emma, stop!" he shouts.

But I don't. Not until I make it to his truck.

"Unlock the door, Jay!" I yell back to him.

The door unlocks immediately, and I hop in the truck, slamming the door behind me. Jay walks slowly to the other side and climbs in.

"Emma." He isn't yelling anymore. He just sounds defeated, and for a moment, we sit in silence until Jay breaks it. "I'm so sorry, Emma. You shouldn't have had to hear that, and it makes me sick to know that you did." He sounds tormented, but I don't say anything, so he continues, "And I wasn't texting Loraine tonight, I promise. There was an emergency at work. A dog that had been hit by a car."

I can't tell if he's telling the truth, but if he is lying,

he's really good at it.

"Just take me home, Jay," I say, unable to find the words or energy to say anything to him right now. I want to scream at him, to cry and tell him I love him. But I can't.

Jay doesn't argue; he just turns on his truck to drive us back to my house.

When we pull onto my street, he doesn't park in the driveway, but on the road, a whole house away from my own, and when he puts the car in park, neither of us attempts to exit the truck or say a word.

My hands are shaking. The tension in here is too much for me to handle and I feel like I am suffocating. After a few minutes, I can't take it anymore and grab the door handle to leave. I just need to be able to *breathe,* and I can't in here with him. But by the time I have the door open mere inches, Jay is leaning over me, pulling it shut again. He doesn't let go of the handle and he doesn't move back to his side of the truck either. His body hovers only inches from mine. After a moment, his forehead meets mine once again. Our mouths so close, I can almost feel his lips on mine. I can smell the wine on his breath. Can feel the pounding of his heart as it matches mine. My eyes flicker to his hand as he lets go of the handle and rests it on my thigh, right where he had earlier. Right where the slit starts. A whimper leaves my mouth before I can stop it, and Jay groans and squeezes my thigh before he moves his hand north to squeeze my hip.

"God, Emma." He breathes. The desire I can hear in his voice makes my mouth water. I want more than anything to taste him. His head moves and his nose slides down my jaw to my neck, and he breathes in a long, deep breath and groans again as if I'm the best thing he's ever smelled.

"What are you doing to me?" he whispers right before he lets his lips make contact with the spot on my neck right below my jaw line. A needy moan escapes me, and I finally move my hands to grab onto his arms as tight as I can, pulling him close to me. His chest pushes up against my breasts, making my nipples harden at the contact. His lips are on me again, this time on my jaw. And then my cheek. And then the corner of my mouth. And then he pulls away so that his lips hover over mine.

Before I have time to let myself think, I close the distance between us. The feel of his mouth on mine after all this time of desire and want... is indescribable. Our mouths collide with each other, almost aggressively, over and over, feeding off one another as if we have been starved. In a way, I guess we have.

His tongue glides over my bottom lip, and I let out another moan, louder this time, and it fills the truck. Jay grabs the middle console and pushes it up so that there's nothing between us anymore. He sits back in his seat but brings me with him, grabbing my legs and pulling them on top of his so that I'm straddling him, just like the other night at his place. And just like the last time I was on top of him, I can feel his hardness beneath me. But unlike last time, he isn't holding back. His hands move over my entire body, grabbing my breasts and then my ass, all while our lips never part. It turns out it wasn't leaving the truck that I needed to be able to breathe again, it was this. It was him.

Our lips finally part, but only so he can move them down to my neck, then up to my ear, and then down to my neck again. This is better than I ever imagined it could be. His hands on my body send waves of pleasure through every inch of me. He pulls down one strap of my dress so that he can pull the fabric below my right breast, freeing me. He hisses and cups it with his hand before he brings his mouth down to it, grabbing my nipple between his teeth gently, but enough to make me cry out in pleasure.

He tugs at the bottom of my dress, pulling it up so that he can reach under it, grabbing onto my thighs with his hands. His fingers roam upward until I can feel his thumb rub over my thong. I push into him.

"Don't stop," I say right as he rubs again. Right over my most sensitive spot.

"Never." He groans in my ear. And with that, his fingers push the small fabric aside and he thrusts two fingers inside me.

"Fuck, Emma, you're so wet." He moans as he pumps his fingers into me over and over.

His thumb moves over my folds and starts making circles, and I can barely control the noises that are coming out of me. His fingers hit just the right spot as he circles over my nub, and I come with a force I have never experienced before. It's like all the tension I have had built up these past few months is finally being released, and it seems to last a glorious amount of time. I ride out the waves of pleasure by grinding into his fingers over and over.

Jay kisses me all over, my neck, my cheek, my nose,

my mouth. I never want it to end because I know I won't recover from this. Now that I know what it's like to have him, I don't know how I will go on without him.

I reach for him this time, wanting to show him the same pleasure he just showed me, but his hand grabs mine, stopping me and pulling it to his face instead, kissing my fingers.

The euphoric feeling that had just filled every ounce of me just moments ago vanishes completely and my heart shatters with the reminder of our reality. It's not my job to pleasure him.

"Why are you with her?" I ask, trying to keep my voice steady, but it comes off as more of a desperate plea.

He sighs. "It's complicated."

"Don't you feel this?" I motion between us. This time I'm unable to hold back the quiver in my voice and the tears that are now forming.

"Of course, I do. And God, Emma, I didn't know she treated you like that, I promise. I would have never been with her in the first place if I knew that's the kind of person she was."

"Well, what about her drinking? She could only hide that for so long. And you had to have realized at some point our relationship wasn't what she was pretending it was." I'm still crying but I need answers from him now, so I force myself to pull it together.

"There were red flags, of course. And after that night at my apartment, I tried to end it. I couldn't deny my feelings for you any longer, but she was hysterical and told me that John had contacted her with threatening messages, and I decided to put my feelings aside, and that your protection was more important. Being with your mother is the only way I can protect you from him."

"Who the fuck is John?" I ask through gritted teeth, trying to contain the anger that's pulsating through me. My heart is pounding out of my chest and my ears are ringing with such a force I'm unsure if he is still talking. My whole body becomes weak, as I let my head fall past him to land on the head rest behind him. *That conniving bitch!*

"What? What are you talking about, Emma? John. Your mom's ex-boyfriend," he explains.

"There has never been a John, Jay," I say to him.

"What?" The color drains from his face.

"There has never been a John. Trust me, I remember each and every one of them. Probably more than she does."

He looks shocked but genuinely confused. "Soon after I started dating your mom, she told me about a man named John that used to beat her. She said that he hit you a few times too and she would try and protect you from him, but he would just lash out and hit her more. She told me that y'all have been terrified of him because he got released from jail earlier this year. That's why I've been over almost every night. And then when I tried to break up with her, she said that John had contacted her and that she was afraid he was going to try and come after the both of you."

All I can do is shake my head and laugh. This is so insane, but it also makes so much sense. No way a man like Jay would have stuck around with her, and she knew that. She came up with the most insane lie and used it to trap him. I have never hated her more than I do in this moment right now.

"There was never a John, Jay. There were lots of others and definitely some that scared me, but none of them ever laid a finger on me. Not because of my mother's protection though. But because since the age of fourteen, I have slept with my door locked and a knife by my bed every single night. I protected myself." I raise my voice this time as I point to myself and let out a sob and then continue. "I protected myself. I cooked my own meals. I got myself to and from school every day and I paid for *everything* I ever wanted. I was my own mother. That woman in there is not a mom nor is she a good person. She isn't even a *decent* person. She is a liar and a drunk. That is all. The only abuse that happened in that house was at her own hands. She is the only reason that I ever felt unsafe in there and it took you too long to see that. And on top of all of that, you stayed with her so you could be, what? Be a father figure to me? That is so messed up. This is *all* so messed up!" Tears stream down my face as I finish declaring everything I have wanted to say since I met Jay. I reach for the door now, needing air to stifle the despair that I'm feeling.

"Emma, please stop!" he begs as he reaches for me.

"No. Let me go and please do not come inside this house tonight," I demand.

He looks at me so helplessly and it breaks me because deep down I know that this is not his fault. I know the only one at fault here is Loraine, that Jay is also a victim of her evil but I can't help how mad I am, and I need to be alone.

"Please, Jay... just go. *Please*," I beg him.

"Okay," he agrees with a whisper and I shut the door and head back to my house with not a clue what is going to happen with us. Or with him and my mother. Or with me and my mother. But one thing is for sure. My mother is more evil than I gave her credit for and I need to get out of this house now more than ever. This house is destroying me and I cannot stay here one second longer.

# Chapter 16

As I stand outside my mother's bedroom door, I fight the urge to pound on it. Part of me wants to wake her ass up and smack her. The other part wants to pack a bag and get the hell out of here and never talk to either of them again. Although I know that last option is not what I *really* want. Especially after what just happened in Jay's truck.

I knew my mother was heartless. I knew she was a terrible mom. I even knew she was a terrible person. But I'm not sure I believed she was capable of such lies and deceit. Mostly because it takes a lot of work to lie like that. And my mother hates work.

Despite it all, I'm just glad that Jay sees her for everything she is now. It was hard making him leave, but I don't think I could have handled seeing them together ever again. Not after everything that just happened. As angry as I am, I can still feel the remnants of pleasure that Jay made me feel just moments ago in his truck. The way his fingers made me feel.

I shake my head, snapping myself back to reality. It doesn't change the fact that Jay stayed with my mom for so long for no reason at all. For a *lie*. Granted, he didn't know it was a lie. But that just means he stuck around so that he could practically act as a father to me. Protecting me from some man that does not even exist. While at the same time making me fall in love with him. That is so messed up. This is all so messed up. And with that thought, I turn around and head to my room to pack a bag, deciding that the best possible answer right now is to get away from both of them and from this terrible, god awful house. Where this whole terrible, god awful mess started.

As I hold my phone to my ear, praying that Jessica is still awake, I start throwing together a bag with clothes and items that will last me the next few days. If I can't stay with Jessica, I will find somewhere to stay. *Anywhere.* Hell, I'll sleep in my car if I have to.

"Emma? You okay?" Jessica picks up, thank goodness. I can hear the concern in her voice, and I'm not surprised because this is the first time I've ever called her.

"Hey, yah. I'm fine, I just…" And in this moment, with the sound of Jessica's comforting and concerned voice, I break. Again. My hand claps over my mouth so that I can somehow control the sobs that come out of me, but now that they have started, I don't know how they'll ever stop. I am a mess.

"Oh, Emma. It's okay. Shhh, it's going to be okay," she comforts me.

"I… I just… I just need a place to stay for a couple of nights," I manage to get out between the sobs.

"Of course. I'm home right now, do you need me to come get you?" she asks.

About an hour ago I would have had to say yes but the events of the past hour have sobered me up.

"No, no, I can drive," I reassure her.

"Okay, I'll text you my address," she tells me.

"Okay, see you soon. Thank you, Jessica."

"Of course, Emma. This is what friends are for." My heart clenches at her comment. Before her, I had never had a friend that would do this for me. Jessica is the only person I can count on right now.

Thirty minutes later, I'm pulling into Jessica's apartment complex. I grab my bag from the front seat and walk up to the apartment number she texted me and knock on the door.

Jessica opens up the door and is holding two pints of ice cream accompanied with the warmest smile. "Get in here, girl," she encourages and hands me one of the pints of cookies and cream. I told her months ago that this was my favorite, I can't believe she remembered. It's impossible not to smile right now.

We spend the next hour talking about what happened and Jessica goes from excited to gushing, back to excitement and then to anger and now to where I'm currently at, shock.

"I cannot believe your mother. Trapping him like that, that is so insane. What a bitch!" Jessica exclaims.

"I know. Part of me isn't surprised at all, but there's still a part of me that has hoped for a long time that there is some good in her. That somewhere down the line something would change. But I know now that it won't. I have no hope when it comes to Loraine anymore."

"I'm sorry, Emma. But family doesn't have to be blood. It's who you make it. I love you and will be here for you always. And it sounds like Jay feels that way too," she encourages and nudges me with her arm and I know she's right. But I still can't get past Jay staying with Loraine for so long, sleeping in her bed with her, having sex with her, being her boyfriend. It's hard to stomach.

"Yah, I know but, God, he stayed with Loraine for longer than he wanted just so he could be some sort of father figure to me, it's all so messed up," I say to her.

"I mean, think about it from his point of view. He starts dating Loraine 'cause he finds her charming and attractive and he thinks it's going to be a fun and easy relationship. Then he meets you and has an undeniable connection. Then she tells him that there's some crazy ex out to get the both of you and the only way to keep you safe is to be at your house every night. The only way he can do that is to stick around with Loraine," she explains and I guess on some level it makes sense. I need to talk to Jay again and hear more from his side. I'm just not even close to being ready to see him again yet.

"I know, but he could have asked me about it. Or ended it with her and offered to help in some other way? I think that just shows that he really did have feelings for Loraine at some point and that thought just makes me sick. How can he have feelings for her *and* me? We are *nothing* alike," I say, emphasizing the nothing.

"Well, I don't think he had feelings for the real Loraine. You saw how much of a show she put on for him. And if he would have never had feelings for the fake Loraine, he would have never met you," she adds and with that, the conversation ends because she is right and even though I hate to think of them together, he was manipulated. And if they wouldn't have ever met, there would be no us and no man has ever made me feel the way Jay has. Yes, I have been acting like a crazy lunatic since he came into my life, but it's not him making my emotions haywire, it is the situation. I vow to myself that I will not see Jay again until the situation changes. Until he and my mother are one hundred and ten percent over and are no longer in any sort of communication. I want to be with him and I want to see where this goes, but I cannot keep putting myself through this.

Jessica has one roommate who is out of town this weekend, thankfully. I can sleep peacefully on her couch without worrying that I'm intruding in anyone else's space. Me and Jessica work the same eleven to four shift at Snaps tomorrow, so I'm thankful to be able to sleep in a little. Even though I'll be sleeping on a couch tonight, I know it will be the best night's sleep I've had in a while because I feel more comfortable here at Jessica's than I have ever felt at Loraine's. That place was never a home to me and from here on out, I won't be referring to it as my home again.

# Chapter 17

My alarm goes off at nine-thirty a.m. and I groan as I roll over on Jessica's couch, feeling the aches in my legs and arms from not being able to sprawl out like I usually do. But still, I feel more rested than I have in a while. I look at my phone and my heart stops when I see a text from Jay.

*"Good morning, Emma. I know you're probably still upset, and you have every right to be. These last few months haven't been easy for you, and I hate that I'm the reason for that. But I just want you to know that even though they haven't been easy for me either, I'm so glad they happened, because they led me to you. I know you need time, but* please *let me explain more. I'm here whenever you're ready. I'll give you as much time as you need."*

I read it over and over and despite all the tears I have cried in the last twenty-four hours, I can't help the butterflies that form in my stomach as I read those words. I'm not ready to face him yet, but I feel the same. These past few months were awful, but I would do them over again a million times if it led me to Jay. I didn't know it was possible to fall in love with someone in such a short period of time, but I have. I love Jay more than I ever believed I could love anyone and it's scary and exciting at the same time.

I type my response, leaving it short and simple, *"I feel the same. I just need a little more time."* And hit send. The three dots pop up that show he's typing but then they disappear and my heart sinks. I remind myself that my text didn't really warrant a response but that doesn't help the brief disappointment I feel right before my phone vibrates.

*"I'll be here. I promise,"* he types. And then another text pops up. *"I ended things with Loraine."*

I hold my phone to my chest and breathe the deepest breath I have had in months. Relief flows through me at the thought of this mess finally being over.

Jessica and I get ready for work and carpool together to our shift. I decide that I still need a little more space to recover emotionally from everything. I want to be clear headed and calm when I see Jay again, so I decide to stay at Jessica's through the rest of the weekend. We both have Sunday off, so we plan to make a girls' day out of it and get our nails done and go to brunch. I have never let myself enjoy a weekend like this and I'm excited to spend some more quality time with my friend. Most of our time spent together has been at work and it feels good to actually hang out.

At brunch the next day, after we have had relaxing pedicures, and order stacks of waffles and bacon paired with bottomless mimosas, I feel lighter than I have in months. I never thought that I needed a friendship like this before, that I was fine being on my own, but I know now that that's not true. Relationships are important. Healthy ones at least.

We get back from brunch and pass out in her bed,

feeling the full effects of those bottomless mimosas. I can't remember the last time I took a nap during the day and it was glorious. We wake up around four and I decide it's time for me to face this mess. I haven't talked to Jay since our texts the previous morning and now that I've decided I'm ready to see him, I'm extremely excited to do that. I have not been able to stop thinking about his lips on mine and I want to feel that again. I want to feel it without anything holding us back. I have no idea what kind of conversation he had with my mother, but I need to hear about that as well. I want everything out in the open. No more lies.

I want to go see Jay right away, but I need to go to Loraine's first. I'm out of fresh clothes and I left my backpack there. At some point tonight, I have to find time to study. I can't let all of this affect graduation. I am too close.

# Chapter 18

When I pull up to the house to see the spot that Jay's truck has occupied these last five months empty, I sigh in relief. I knew it wouldn't be there. He already told me they broke up. But I'm so used to being on edge every time I've pulled up to this house these last three months, it's hard to break that feeling. I gulp as I enter the front door, anxious to what kind of state my mother will be in. When I make my way to the living room, I find Loraine lying on the couch, barely holding on to a wine glass, some drops have already spilled on the carpet. Her eyes are glued to the TV, but I can tell by the redness and puffiness she's been crying.

There is no part of me that aches or feels sorry for her. I'm not an evil person, but right now the only feelings I have looking down at my distraught mother is pure joy. I'm not sure what that makes me, but I really don't care.

"Where have you been?" she asks me sharply and I am taken aback. She has never once asked me about my whereabouts before. Part of me is curious about what she knows or what she is assuming right now based on her hostile tone. I don't think she would ever actually physically harm me, but if she's drunk enough, and assumes something has happened between me and her ex-boyfriend, could she snap? I decide that I really don't know the answer to that so I tread carefully with my words.

"At my friend Jessica's," I say, keeping my tone neutral.

"You don't have any friends," she spits out, but I ignore the harsh statement because she knows absolutely nothing about me, let alone whether or not I have friends.

"You okay?" I ask her, only because I want nothing more than for her to have to tell me out loud that Jay dumped her. And if she relives any of that pain, even better.

She barely looks over at me as just manages to mumble, "Jay broke up with me."

It takes everything in me not to smile right in her face as she shares the news. I'm careful with what I say next, because I'm not sure what all Jay has said to her. I doubt he told her anything about us, which means she may not realize that Jay found out that John was a complete lie. But I want her to at least know she deserves what she got.

"Well, honestly, Mother, you put on quite a show for him, I'm sure it was exhausting for you." This won't give anything away because John was not the only lie she told. I had to watch her pretend to be a caring mother multiple times and let's be honest, that was the greatest lie of them all. It was exhausting just to watch; I cannot imagine how tiring it was for her to do all that acting. Surely, she has to feel some sort of relief now that she doesn't have to put on a show anymore.

"Excuse me?" she asks, this time sitting up on the couch to finally look at me. She has no makeup on, her eyes are tired and red, and her hair is a mess. I have never seen her look this rough and it makes me feel good. I stand taller knowing out of the two of us right now, I am the more beautiful one. I know thinking that should make me feel awful. But it doesn't.

"Was it not exhausting pretending to be something you're not?"

"Get out of my face," she snaps as she grabs her glass of wine and storms to her room, slamming the door behind her.

It feels good to stand up to her. To call her ass out. I feel confident and proud of myself and now all I want is to see Jay. I pull out my phone to text him to ask if I can come over and then hop in the shower. When I get out, I have two texts from him. One saying, *"I'd love that"* and the other telling me his address. I smile and even though I'm anxious to see him, I take some time to make myself look good. I throw on fitted jeans and a tight, brown, long-sleeve shirt that shows off my breasts. I do a light makeup look, blow dry my hair and let it hang over my shoulders, and then pack a new bag with enough clothes to last me a few days.

I don't know if I'll be staying at Jay's, although I really hope so. Either way, I know I won't be staying here. Graduation is so close now I can practically taste it, but it is still too long of a time to stay here. Especially now. If I can't stay with Jay, maybe I can stay with Jessica. But my time in this house has come to an end. Quicker than I planned and I am in no way financially prepared to move out, but I will figure something out. I will worry about that tomorrow. Right now, all I want to do is go see the man that I love. Grabbing my bag and my school stuff, I head to my car, feeling more excited and at peace than I have in a long time.

When I arrive at Jay's door, some of the confidence I felt just moments ago falters and I find myself a little nervous and have to wipe the sweat off my palms and onto my jeans. But the minute he opens the door and I see him standing before me, looking delicious in gray sweats and a plain black tee that emphasizes his toned arms, the nerves I feel vanish. He swiftly pulls me into him and wraps his arms around me, engulfing me into him, and I relish in this feeling. This is the first time that Jay has touched me without the looming thoughts of him and my mother lingering between us and it feels good. It feels right. Like his arms were made to hold me like this. Like my body was made to fit perfectly into his embrace.

He lets me go, but just long enough to grab my bags from me and set them in the kitchen, and then he immediately pulls me back into him again. I melt into him and soak up everything about this moment. The way his lips feel as he plants kisses on the top of my head. The smell of his cologne, woody and fruity on his shirt, as I breathe him in. The warmth of his skin as he holds me tight against him. Everything outside of this embrace disappears and I hold on to him for dear life, anxious to put everything we've been through behind us and move forward.

"I'm so glad you're here," he tells me, his breath hitting the skin on my neck and it reminds me of the other night, sending a shiver down my spine.

"Me too," I say as I pull away just enough so that I can see him. To *really* see him. To be able to take all of him in and appreciate his beauty for the first time. God, he is gorgeous. But as much as I want to stare at him forever, we need to talk. We need to get everything out in the open so that we can move on. Together.

"You broke up with her?" I ask even though I already know the answer, and he pulls me over to the couch so we can sit together.

"Of course. I don't love her; I never did and I should have ended it a long time ago. I thought I was doing the right thing by staying with her for so long. I should have talked to you sooner about John, especially after what happened with that guy Landon. But your mother said you hated talking about it." He shakes his head in anger at the mention of another one of Loraine's lies.

"But besides all of that, the minute I started falling in love with you, I should have ended it with her. I am so sorry for putting you through that for so long," he says as he squeezes my hands and brings them up to his mouth, leaving gentle kisses on them.

"You love me?" I ask, shocked. I mean, I've known that I've loved him for a while now. Of course, I knew he liked me, but to hear the word love come out of his mouth, to know that he feels the same way that I do, makes everything we have gone through worth it.

"I do. A lot," he answers matter-of-factly.

"I love you too. These past few months have been awful, but sitting here with you now, I know they were worth it." I know the situation he was in must have been awful and awkward, just as it was for me.

"Come here," he says as he pulls me to him, bringing

his mouth to mine. There was so much negativity still lingering in the background of our make-out session in his truck Friday night, but this kiss is different. There is nothing between us anymore. There is nothing but the two of us and the start of something new. Something *amazing.*

He breaks the kiss and he can sense my disappointment instantly.

"Look, Lorraine and I, we haven't had sex in a while. I want you to know that. Not since I knew that what I was feeling for you was real. I stuck around because I thought I was protecting you, but I dodged her every attempt in bed."

I didn't realize how heavy the weight of that worry had felt on me until he said those words. For so long, I wondered how he could be sleeping with her and having intimate moments with me but before I can say anything, he continues. "But with all that you told me about her... all the men... it really concerns me and before we can really be together in that way, I want to make sure I'm clean. We always used a condom, but I want to be absolutely sure. I got tested on Friday and should have all my results in the next couple of days. I want nothing from Loraine lingering between us, okay?" he tells me as he cups my face in his palms and I nod because one, the continued talk of him and Loraine being intimate together needs to end now, and two, he is right. As badly as I want Jay right now, I know it's better to be safe we have waited this long to be together, what is a few more days? "You're right, thank you for doing that. And just so you know, I haven't been with anyone since the last time I was tested

134

at my checkup," I add.

He nods and then combines our mouths again for another delicious but torturous kiss. The way his lips move against mine so perfectly make it feel as if they were made for each other and I can't believe this is what I've been missing out on the last few months.

"I can't wait to be with you." I break from his mouth just long enough to whisper that to him. He brings his forehead down to mine and groans and I know he is feeling just as tortured as I am right now.

"Emma, I haven't stopped thinking about being inside you since the last time you were here. The feeling of you on me, it races through my head every minute of every day and it's all I think about before I go to sleep each night." He breathes.

"Me too."

He pulls me in for one more deep kiss, slower this time, and my tongue slides along his lower lip and he groans but then separates us. "Please don't torture me," he begs and I giggle.

"I want you to stay here with me, okay? I don't want you ever staying there again. There may not have been an actual John, but what you told me about sleeping with your door locked and a knife by your bed? That haunts me. I want you here with me, okay?"

My heart swells. No one has ever taken care of me like this. It's not in a parental way like I had feared. Just a loving way. A way I would imagine anyone wanting to protect a loved one would act. I think back to what Jessica said about family is who you make it, and even though my circle is small, literally two people, I feel like I really do have a family. After being alone my whole life, I feel more love from these two than I ever thought I would from anyone.

"Okay," I say as tears fall down my cheeks. God, it feels good to finally be crying tears of *joy.*

He wipes them away from my face, kissing the trails they make, and I feel more at home here in his arms than I ever have in my entire life.

"Emma..." He pauses after my name as if he's nervous to continue but eventually, he does. "I can't stop thinking about what you said Friday night. That you heard Loraine and I and... I don't even know what to say really, other than I'm so incredibly sorry and that if I knew you were home, I would have never... I hate myself for putting you through that and I don't know if it helps, but I'd guess what you heard was the last time and it hadn't happened for a while before that either and—"

"Stop," I say before he can continue because I don't want to talk or think about it ever again and this moment is too good to be ruined by that memory. "Let's just move on and never talk or think about it again, okay? I promise I'm not mad at you for it, I just really, *really* want to never have to think about it again," I tell him.

He nods his head. "I like that plan. Now come on, let's make dinner," he says as he stands and grabs my hand.

"What are we having?" I ask, excited to experience something *normal* with Jay for the first time.

"Chicken alfredo and garlic bread. Nothing fancy, but my mom made it for us all the time when we were growing up and it is definitely a favorite of mine. I cook it every week," he says as my mouth waters at the thought of it.

This is it. This is what I've wanted my whole life. To be out of that house, to have a family, and to feel free. All of these feelings are hitting me at once and it's unlike any feeling I have ever felt before. It feels euphoric and I never want it to end.

My whole life I have never had time to worry about being happy and enjoying the moment. My life was only about survival. About learning how to cook so I didn't starve. About learning how to protect myself from any predators my mother decided to bring home to her bed. About growing a tough skin to handle any nasty comments made from Loraine. About studying my ass off every minute I could so I could get good grades to attend a good college and then when I got to college, I studied even harder.

Never once was I ever truly happy. Never once did I ever stop and enjoy the moment or enjoy the people around me. Not until this weekend. Not until my weekend with Jessica and this moment right here with Jay. I have no idea how to describe what I am feeling other than pure happiness, and I am feeling it for the first time in my entire life at the age of twenty-one.

# Chapter 19

The rest of the night is spent with me giving him every detail of what it was like growing up under Loraine's roof. I tell him all about how I have been taking care of myself since I can remember, about the type of guys Loraine would bring home, and especially about Ben. Telling Jay about Ben trying to get into my bedroom when I was just fourteen was more difficult than I thought it would be. Besides Loraine, no one knew about that night. I had never spoken about it out loud since and I find it extremely hard. The thought of what *could* have happened that night, but didn't, terrifies me. I want to cry for that scared little girl all alone, holding a knife in her room in case she had to protect herself.

Jay is furious as I recount the memory, and after what he did to Landon, I am pretty sure if he ever ran into Ben, it would be very, very bad. He is also furious with Loraine. The more I tell him about her, the *real* her, the her that Jay didn't know existed, the angrier he becomes. It's hard to miss the look of regret on his face. The frown line that creases between his eyes like he can't stop thinking about something awful and I can tell by the way he looks at me that he is taking some of the blame.

"Hey, she's deceiving, it is *not* your fault, you were used and manipulated," I remind him.

"It doesn't feel like that. I should have seen through her bullshit. I'm so sorry, Emma," he apologizes, his head dropping into his hands as if he's in agony.

"Hey, it's okay. I promise. None of this is your fault," I assure him. "And besides, I'm tough," I say with a smile that I hope can relax him down a little. He smiles back at me.

"I'm just so happy to be here with you right now," I add as I grab his hand from across his kitchen table. He squeezes my hand in response and then brings it to his mouth, brushing his lips over my skin.

"I'm curious, though; what all did you tell Loraine when you ended things?" I ask him.

"I told her that the way she spoke to you that night was revolting and that her drinking was not something I wanted to be a part of and that she clearly wasn't the woman she pretended to be. I didn't tell her anything about us. I didn't think you'd want her to know and if you did, I figured it should be on your terms. I'll go with you if that's something you decide you want to do," he tells me sincerely.

"No. I'm done with her. I don't care to tell her. It's not something I feel like I need to do. I'm ready to put her behind me once and for all," I state and I mean it.

"Then that's what we'll do," he replies.

"Oh, by the way, she was never a lawyer. That was so hard for me not to tell you." I laugh because of how utterly ridiculous that lie was and I had completely forgotten about it until this very moment.

Jay shakes his head in annoyance. "I'm not surprised

at this point. Why didn't you just tell me?" he asks.

"I wanted you to see her for who she truly is on your own. I wanted it to be on her, not on me," I express.

He brings my bags into his room and then takes me on a tour of his two-bedroom, two-bath apartment complex. It's a nice apartment in a nice area of Houston, and it is obvious he makes decent money in his career as a vet. Although none of that money seems to go towards decorating this place. This is most definitely a man's apartment. It is extremely minimal, with only the absolute necessities.

"This is my room, and bathroom and then down this hall is the second bathroom and the bedroom you stayed in last time," he says as he walks me down the hallway, my hand in his.

"It was so hard not to just let you stay in my room. I just wanted to hold you after what happened that night," he admits.

As I take in the room, all the memories from that night come flooding back to me.

"Thanks for taking care of me. That night was really awful and could have been so much worse if it weren't for you."

Anger flashes through his face at the memory of the night. "I'm not sure I've ever gotten so close to going to jail than that night. I wanted to kill him." I can tell by his tone as he says this that he means it.

I want to lighten the mood and put that terrible memory behind us so I laugh as I ask a question I have been dying to know the answer to. "Did you change me that night?" I ask with a teasing tone.

"More so just helped you. You were kind of in and out of consciousness, but for the most part you were able to throw on my clothes yourself." He chuckles before he adds, "But don't worry, I didn't see anything. I promise. I turned around when you didn't have your clothes on."

"It would have been okay if you saw me," I admit.

"No, I would not have looked at you without your permission, Emma."

I swoon at his words, the most gentlemanly words any man has ever said to me. As more memories from that night start to come to the surface, it is hard not to think about what happened between us in the kitchen.

"That night with you was intense." The image of me straddling him is so strong in my head right now I can practically feel him underneath me just as I had that night.

"It was. It changed everything for me," he says as he wraps his arms around me from behind and rests his chin on my shoulder. "The moment you said you were going on a date, I knew. I knew that I wanted you. That I *needed* you. That I didn't want you to be with anyone else but me," he growls in my ear.

His voice ripples down my body. His words alone unravel me, but that paired with his body wrapped around mine and the images from that night have me aching for him. I know we can't have sex, but I want him as turned on as I am right now.

"I touched myself that night. While wearing your boxers. After you told me to go back to the room," I confess.

His body hardens behind mine and he lets out a groan in my ear. My core throbs in response.

"Emma," he grumbles.

"I was pretty loud, I thought maybe you heard me."

"I did," he confesses and I turn to face him, shocked this is the first time he's admitting to this. He continues, "I had to lock myself in my room to stop myself from joining you. And then I got in the shower and did the exact same thing to myself," he says sexily, nuzzling his nose in my neck and kissing me in the exact right spot.

"Why didn't you say anything?" I ask.

"I didn't know if I was supposed to hear," he says.

"You were," I say as my eyes lock on his and his hands start to roam over my body.

My body heats up and part of me wants to say fuck it and have sex right now. But I don't want anything between us when we get to take that step for the first time. No condoms and definitely no worrying that Loraine could have given something to Jay.

"When do you get those results again?"

"Not soon enough. Hopefully by Tuesday," he answers, kissing my neck in just the right spot that makes my toes curl.

"We've waited this long. What's a couple more days?"

"Exactly. Come on, let's go to bed before we change our minds." He pulls away from me and I grin when I see his erection through his pants. Thank God for gray sweatpants. They leave nothing to the imagination.

We get ready for bed and I throw on my tank top and

pajama shorts and I laugh 'cause I really don't mean to torment him anymore, but with the way my nipples poke through my top and my ass cheeks hang out of my bottoms, I already know it's going to be a torturous night for the both of us.

"Are you kidding me?" he says as he comes out of the bathroom and sees me sitting on his large king bed in my scandalous pajamas.

"I'm sorry I just grabbed my usual pajamas!" I laugh.

"Don't be sorry one bit, baby," he says and I am practically melting at his use of the term "baby." He gets in bed and I climb in beside him under the covers, closing the distance between us. He pulls me tightly to him and I squeal when he squeezes one of my ass cheeks with his strong hand. He laughs and squeezes harder, making me giggle even more. But when his hand stops squeezing my butt and moves north to squeeze my breast, his thumb rubbing over my hard nipple that is poking through the thin material, all laughter stops. His large hand cups my breast perfectly.

"That feels so good." I breathe as his thumb rubs over me again.

He squeezes again and I moan, arching my back so I push my breast more into his grasp. Jay bites his lip and groans, "Fuck, I want you." But just as I think he is about to continue, he comes back to reality, removes his hand and pulls me down to cuddle on his chest. The hand that was just teasing me, now rubbing circles on my arm.

"Let's go to sleep. Maybe the results will be in tomorrow. They better be because I don't know how much longer I can wait to be inside you," he declares and my groin clenches in response to his words.

I turn my body around and let Jay be the big spoon. He wraps himself around me and our bodies mold together perfectly, just like our lips did earlier. I let myself savor this feeling. The feeling of falling asleep somewhere safe and happy. No alcoholic mother, no strange men, no knives or locked bedroom doors. Jay's apartment already feels more like a home than Loraine's house ever did, and I drift off to sleep without a worry in the world.

# Chapter 20

Jay's results from the doctor did not come in on Monday unfortunately. I am telling myself it's a good thing because I know once we are finally able to have sex, it's all I am going to want to do and all I am going to think about every second of every day and although I know it will be amazing, I still have school to think about. I may have gotten out of my mother's house earlier than planned, but that has not changed my goals. I have been counting down the days until I'm a college graduate for as long as I can remember and I have worked so damn hard these past three and half years, I will not let anything get in the way of walking across that stage and getting my diploma. And besides, I make nowhere near enough at Snaps to help with rent, and even though Jay insists it's okay, I do not feel okay about it. I am thrilled to be living with Jay, but I want to contribute to a home that we share so finding a big girl job is number one on my to-do list.

I spend the entire day giving school my undivided attention. I study between classes and then when my classes are done, I head to Snaps where I study for four more hours before my night shift starts at four p.m. Then, when I get off at nine p.m. and head back to Jay's apartment, I find him waiting for me with open arms and gives me a hug that I wish I could bottle up and keep forever. We spend the rest of the night cuddling on the couch, our limbs tangled together as we laugh at the silly comedy movie on the TV. There are no orgasms to be had, but I could argue that the feeling of this moment is just as good. Well maybe not *as* good, but I do love it very much.

Tuesday is a lot of the same, a morning full of studying and classes and then later I'll work the afternoon shift with Jessica. It's only been a couple days since I've seen her, but it feels like forever because so much has happened since then. She has been texting me non-stop, begging for details about Jay, and I promised her I would tell her everything today.

She practically tackles me as she runs in for our shift and I can't help but smile at how excited she is to hear about my life. I get her all caught up on everything, even though it takes forever because we have to keep pausing to take orders and make coffees. But eventually, she is up to speed with everything and seems genuinely happy for me. Which in turn only makes me even happier.

It is just about three o'clock when I feel my phone vibrate. My heart speeds up because I know Jay should be getting his results today and I have been extremely anxious waiting to hear from him.

The text is from Jay and it's an image, but I hesitate to open it. I'm praying that there is nothing from Loraine lingering between us and we can finally move forward. But I tell myself if not, it will be okay. *We* will be okay. We will get through whatever comes our way.

With shaky fingers I click on Jay's text to open the picture. The image pulls up and it is definitely his results from the doctor. Every Sexually Transmitted Infection is listed and has a "negative" next to each one.

I let out an audible sigh and Jessica turns around to look at me. "What is it?"

I show her my phone screen, since I just told her minutes ago that we were waiting for this, and she gives me a devilish grin. "Oh, girl, it is on tonight!" she teases and my cheeks go hot, and I really, *really* need the next two hours to fly by.

Jay sent another text under the image that reads, *"See you tonight, baby"* with a winking emoji face and I can barely breathe.

*"I'm so relieved to see that! Counting down the minutes!"* I type back, adding the kissy emoji with it.

The last two hours of work, of course, are slammed. The busyness makes the time go by faster, but I am so antsy to get out of here, I have dropped one cup of milk and had to redo two orders which is so unlike me. All I can think about is getting home to Jay and feeling every inch of him on every inch of me.

Five o'clock finally rolls around and I practically speed home. Jay doesn't get home until five-thirty, so I will have just enough time to freshen up before he gets home.

Quickly, I open the door with the key he gave me and run to the bathroom. I hop in the shower to do a quick rinse of my body and make sure everything is groomed and cleaned up. My hair gets pulled up in a high pony, because that's the hairstyle that makes me feel the most powerful and sexy, and I retouch my makeup just a smidge. I pull out the silk pajama set I brought that Jay hasn't seen yet. It's silky and spaghetti strapped with lace lining the top above the chest line, and more lace lining the bottom of the shorts. The silk and lace are both black and with how much he likes my plain boring pajamas, I already know he is going to love these. The material is thin and I go with no bra, so you can see my nipples perfectly and my cleavage busts out of the top.

I finish in perfect timing because right when I'm walking back to the living room, Jay is opening the front door. He stops when he sees me and then drops his work bag on the table and rushes toward me, his arms around me in seconds, his mouth slamming into mine.

"God, you're beautiful." He groans as our mouths collide with one another.

His hand makes its way from my back to my breast and he squeezes, cupping me with his hand and I whimper. I'll never get over how my size C breast fits perfectly in the grasp of his big hand.

He pulls away for just a second to say, "I smell like dog." And we both start cracking up.

"I don't care," I tell him and pull his mouth back to mine, not willing to wait a second longer.

He lifts me up and I wrap my legs around his waist as he carries us to his room, our mouths never parting. He lays me carefully on the bed and hovers over me, bringing his mouth back down to mine as our hands start to explore one another's bodies. One of his hands goes back to my breast, and then his fingers trail to my nipple, pinching it over the thin fabric in just the right way that I think the sensation alone could make me come.

My hands go to his ass and I pull him into me so that I can feel him against me. He is wearing jeans, but I can still feel how ready he is for me through the thick denim. Things move quickly after that. I help him remove his polo and then in seconds my hands are on his buckle, hastily undoing the metal. I get his buckle and pant buttons undone and then he pulls off my silk top, the cool apartment air hits my bare skin. He stops for just a second to admire me, he has never seen me bare like this, and I relish in his look. After a few moments, we are back to moving frantically as he helps me remove his pants, neither of us having the patience to take things slow right now. Not after all this time.

He pulls his jeans off and I can see how big he is through his boxers. How ready he is for me and just when I'm about to reach up to feel him, he guides me back down on the bed. My breathing is heavy and the anticipation is killing me. I want to feel him. Now. But he slows things down, taking his time now as he pulls down my bottoms.

"I love you so much," he says as he looks down at me lying under him, fully naked and exposed.

"I love you too," I manage to whisper.

His mouth makes contact with my inner thigh and he slowly plants kisses up my leg, making his way up to the spot that has been throbbing for his attention for weeks. I squirm under him, enjoying every second, but also wanting him to move faster. Eventually, his mouth makes contact right where I need it to, and I cry out at the immense pleasure of it.

His tongue starts making circles on my flesh and after a few seconds, I am completely soaked and begging him. "Jay. Please. I need you. I need you inside me," I plead as I pull him up and reach for his length. He groans as I push my hands inside his boxers and wrap my fingers around him. He is rock hard and I don't think either of us will make it long once we get started.

He gets his boxers off rapidly and lowers himself back on top of me and I feel the tip of him at my opening and I can't take it anymore. I plead with him again and raise my hips to his, trying to get him inside me, and I can feel the smirk on his lips on my mouth as he pulls back, torturing me.

"Jay, pleaseeeee," I pant as I grab his waist to try and pull him into me, but he is stronger than me and stays hovering where he's at, the tip of his length pushing no more than a centimeter into me. I have never needed anything more in my life.

"Shhhh, baby," he whispers as he moves his lip to my ear. "I want to soak up every second of this," he says right before he bites my ear, making me whine. He pushes in another inch, but then pulls back again and I cry out, the desire is almost painful.

"Jay, I need you," I cry.

"You have me," he responds as he slowly enters me more, maybe two inches this time, but it is still not enough and I practically sob when he pulls out again.

"God, you're so wet." He groans as he glides inside me more this time. Enough that it finally releases some of the pressure that has been building. He pulls back again and then finally thrusts all of him into me and a noise, that is closer to a scream than a moan, escapes from deep within me.

"Fuck!" he growls, and he thrusts in me again, unable to control himself any longer.

He pulls out just enough again so that he can flip me onto my hands and knees and in less than a second, he's pumping into me again. The position we're in has him hitting a spot deep inside me no man has ever reached before.

"Touch yourself," he moans in my ear as he grabs one of my hands and pushes it down my stomach. "Just like you did in the other room."

I do as he says and start working my fingers in quick circles over my folds. The combination of him inside me with my fingers puts me over the edge.

"I'm going to come," I whimper.

"Come for me, baby."

And I do. Waves of pleasure course through me, reaching into my toes and I think my eyes might have even rolled to the back of my head.

I can tell that Jay is close too and I want to feel him when he climaxes, so I tell him, "Come inside me, I'm on the pill." And in seconds, he's letting go and releasing every last bit of him into me, just as the last few waves of ecstasy finish flowing through me.

He holds me afterward, both of us breathless and in a state of bliss. Finally, after Jay has caught his breath and is able to speak, "I'm sorry that took so long. I hope the wait was worth it." He teases as he kisses the top of my head.

"Every minute," I reassure him. And it was. I'm not surprised sex with Jay is the best I've ever experienced and I can already feel the buzz of want reforming in my body.

As we lie there, I notice the scar on Jay's stomach again and do what I wanted to do the last time I saw it. "I saw this that day you stopped me in the hallway after we had stayed up talking the night before. I wanted to reach out and do this," I say as my finger traces the raised skin. "What happened?" I asked.

"You're gonna laugh," he says with a smile.

I sit up, instantly more curious now. "Tell me!" I laugh.

"See, you're already laughing!"

"Oh my gosh, you're killing me, now I *have* to know!" I exclaim.

"Okay, okay! It's from a cat," he says.

I do laugh. "A cat?"

"Hey, in my defense, it was a very angry cat that was brought in with her babies. We wanted to keep them all together and when I went to pick up the first kitten, mom lost it and went after me, her long nail ripped straight through my shirt!"

I smile at that. "Sounds like a good momma," I say.

"Come here," he says as he pulls me back down to him.

We lie there in silence for a few minutes, my hand still tracing Jay's scar, his hand rubbing my back.

"What are you thinking about?" I ask after a while, curious what is going on in his head.

"That morning. How sexy you looked, fresh out of

152

your bed in those tiny pajamas. The way your nipples poked through that practically see-through tank top. God, I couldn't get you out of my head all day," he admits.

I sit up. "I have a confession."

"Oh yah?" he asks as he raises his eyebrows, curiosity etched across his face.

"In your guest bedroom isn't the only time I thought about you while I touched myself. I was so worked up after that moment in the hallway, I masturbated in the shower," I confess.

His eyes burn through me, the need and want in them so strong I ache for him all over again. "Fuck, Emma. How did we go so long without one another?" he says as he pulls me down onto him and we make love again, taking our time this time and exploring every inch of each other.

Eventually, we pull ourselves out of his bed so that we can eat dinner, but it isn't long before we're intertwined with one another again. And then, in the early morning hours, we find ourselves connected again for the fourth time.

It was the best night of my life.

# Chapter 21

It's nearly impossible to wake up the next morning. Which is understandable since we didn't get much sleep. Jay's arms fold over me, engulfing me. I can feel his chest rise and fall against my back and his warmth seeps through me like the way a warm cup of coffee does on a cold day. I never want to get out of this bed. Especially because today is the day I'm going to go back to my mother's to get the rest of my stuff.

After my classes this morning, I have the rest of the afternoon to pack up because I took the day off from Snaps. I'm anxious to get my things and be done with that house once and for all, but I have been so elated these past few days I'm terrified that going back to that environment is going to be like a black hole, sucking out all the joy that has been charging through me since Friday. On top of this, my mother is going to have questions. She may not usually care about my life, but moving out is a pretty big deal and I imagine she is not just going to sit there quietly as I do it. Especially since it's happening directly after I go to a fancy event with Jay and then he breaks up with her. Maybe I'm just paranoid, but I feel like she has to at least be a little suspicious. She may be a drunk, but she isn't stupid.

Eventually, we have to pull ourselves out of the bed

because Jay has an important surgery at nine and I need to get ready to head to my first class.

We linger too long at my car and I know we are both going to be running late, but Jay is planting sweet kisses on my lips, neither of us wanting to say goodbye now that we are finally together, and it is nearly impossible to part from him.

Finally, we go our separate ways and I pull up to campus right at nine and by the time I walk to my building, I'm five minutes late and all heads turn to me, including the professor's, as the old door creaks shut behind me. I cringe in embarrassment, but I'm not regretful. Those extra five minutes of Jay's lips on mine are worth all the embarrassment.

My last class today ends right before noon and even though I'm dreading what comes after it, the morning seems to fly by. Why is it that when you are excited for something, time seems to tick by in slow motion, but when it's the opposite, there seems to be no time at all?

Before I know it, I am pulling back into my mother's driveway, hands slightly trembling and despite every ounce of me yearning to be this brave woman who can hold her head high in a moment like this, there are nearly twenty-two years of pain flashing through my mind right now. Every lonely, miserable memory makes me want to turn this car around and say fuck it, I can just buy all new things. But, regardless of my fear, I know that I need this. This is the only way I can get full closure and truly put this place and Loraine behind me.

I walk to the front door and I feel like a stranger here

now. In a way, I guess I always have. It has only been three days since I was last here, but so much has happened in that short time. It feels like an entire lifetime ago. *I can do this,* I think to myself. *Just throw as much shit in your car that will fit and get out of here.*

My pulse quickens as my hand turns the doorknob and my mind tries one last time to talk me out of it, to just leave and come back tonight when I know Loraine will be passed out, but I push that thought down quickly before it can convince me, and open the door. I can do this.

When I enter the living area, I see Loraine right where I found her on Sunday. Lying on the couch with a drink in her hand. Except this time, it's not wine, it's straight vodka and the handle that is nearly gone is sitting on the coffee table. She is up, barely, and her eyes are glued to the TV. They stay that way even when I shut the door behind me.

"Hey," I say, but she doesn't acknowledge me. She doesn't even blink and if she wasn't clutching the glass of vodka in her hand for dear life, I would think she was dead.

I give up and walk past her into my bedroom, realizing I may be able to get through this without any interaction with her and that thought has me moving faster than a freight train. I throw my purse down on my desk and start shoving as many clothes and shoes as possible into my laundry basket. I close the lid and pile the rest of my school books on top of it and then pick it up by the openings on the side and carry it to my car, passing Loraine in the same position on the couch that she was in five minutes ago.

I dump everything into my trunk, including all of the clothes and shoes that are in the laundry basket, so that I can go in and fill it up again. It is not efficient by any means and definitely going to be a pain in the ass to unload, but I don't own luggage and I also did not want to go buy a bunch of boxes so this will have to do. Besides, it may be a mess, but this is probably the fastest way.

Grabbing the laundry basket, I head back inside to load it up again. I make my way into the house and back into the living room area but stop dead in my tracks when I see that Loraine is no longer on the couch and her drink is sitting on the coffee table next to the handle of vodka.

My breath quickens and I try not to panic, but I have no idea what to expect from her behavior right now. I keep my guard up as I slowly make my way back to my room. I turn into the doorway and then stop abruptly when I see Loraine at my desk, holding herself up with one hand and scrolling through my phone with the other. All color drained from her face. The basket slips from my fingers and falls to the ground as I stare at her in shock. I have been alone my whole life, never did I have to worry about putting a password on my phone, but I am mentally reprimanding myself right now. Kicking myself for leaving my phone that is full of evidence that Jay and I are together, sitting right here in this room for her to find. I knew she would probably be suspicious. What had I been thinking? Neither of us say a word and a part of me wonders if she has even noticed me standing here.

Eventually, after what feels like an endless amount of time, she breaks the silence with an uncontrollable laughter. Because she's extremely intoxicated and barely able to stand, it comes out wrong. Not sounding like a normal laugh at all, instead more like a cackle. Almost evil. Like what you would imagine a witch sounded like. She has always been a witch in my eyes, but she has never really looked like one. She has never looked evil, although that is what she is on the inside. Not until now. Right now, looking at her as she laughs hysterically, a wild look in her eyes, I find myself actually frightened of her for the first time in my life.

"Give me my phone, Loraine," I demand, using the sternest voice that I can muster up despite the lump in my throat.

"You fuckin' my boyfriend?" she spits at me while still holding the feral smile on her face, the terrifying cackle that just filled the room is now gone and we're surrounded by silence.

The audacity she has to call him her boyfriend dissolves any fear I had. Instead, it brings back every ounce of anger I felt Friday night when I had learned of all the lies she told Jay. Of the way she manipulated him into staying with her.

"Your boyfriend? Really? He's not your boyfriend anymore, Loraine, and honestly, he never was," I snap back at her, trying to control the fury boiling inside of me. I want to hurt her right now. I want to take the frame that is hanging on the wall next to me and chunk it at her face. I have never felt this sort of rage before.

"And whose fault is that!" she shrieks.

"You lied to him, Mother! John? How did you even come up with that ridiculous sob story? You are something else. And a retired lawyer? That is hilarious. He may have fallen in love with me, but he NEVER loved you, Mother. There is no amount of lies that could EVER make someone love you!" I scream back at her, allowing every ounce of anger and hurt that I have ever felt toward her spill out of me.

"You have taken EVERYTHING from me!" She starts to cry, tears pouring down her face now, and even though I have never seen her cry before, I feel nothing. No regret, no pity, nothing, just pure hatred.

"Me? Are you serious? I have NEVER asked you for anything! I have never taken a DAMN thing from you and I certainly didn't ask you to get pregnant with me at fifteen. YOU DID THAT YOURSELF!" I scream and it is my turn to cry now. The tears are uncontrollable and I hate myself for them, but I can't stop them. They aren't out of sadness, just anger.

Her eyes widen at that last comment and she snaps and screams, "GET OUT OF MY HOUSE, YOU SLUT!" She throws my phone across the bedroom into the wall.

I can barely see straight, red and blur filling my vision, but I manage to reach past her and grab my bag. Part of me thinks she may hit me. Part of me even wants her to because then I can hit her back. But she doesn't. Quickly, I grab my phone from the floor and walk to my car. I want more than anything to sprint out of this house, but I do not want to give her the satisfaction of thinking she has scared me, even if she has a little bit, so I hold my head as high as I can and walk away from her knowing it will be the last time.

My phone is done for. I try to turn it on, but the screen

is shattered, and it stays black despite me continuously holding down the power button. I need Jay right now, but I can't even call him. It's one o'clock which means he's probably on his lunch break, but I don't know how to get to his clinic and since my phone isn't working, I can't Google it.

Finally, after some few deep breaths, I manage to put the car in drive and head back to Jay's apartment. Tears still fall down my face as I make my way in the door, but even though I can't seem to stop crying, I feel numb. I have a lot of awful memories with Loraine but never once in my life have we fought like that, or has she called me a slut. It was the perfect ending to the era that my life has been. The perfect storm. It was not the closure I wanted, but it was closure nonetheless. I am drained and barely make it to the couch, collapsing on the sofa cushions and curling up into the fetal position.

When I really think about it, I feel nothing toward Loraine anymore. Not even anger. There is nothing left to feel. It's all gone. But for some reason, I can't stop the tears. They just won't stop. Not until I eventually cry myself to sleep on Jay's couch.

# Chapter 22

I wake to the feeling of a warm and gentle hand on my back and open my eyes to see Jay sitting on the couch next to me. My eyes are puffy and swollen, I can tell the minute I open them, and every inch of my head throbs from behind my eyes all the way down to the back of my neck.

"Hey, baby," he says softly as he rubs circles on my back.

"What time is it?" I croak, my throat raspy from the screaming and crying.

"About three o'clock," he says as he tucks a hair behind my ear and leans down to plant kisses on my swollen eyes. My eyes close immediately in response because for a brief moment, it dulls the ache that is pulsing behind them.

"What happened?" he asks.

I sit up but have to move my hand to my head because the throbbing returns with a vengeance at the movement.

"Did she hurt you?" he asks, sounding panicked.

"No. No, I just have a terrible headache; do you have any medicine?" I ask.

"Yes, of course, stay here," he tells me and is back in minutes with a glass of water and two Tylenol.

I swallow the Tylenol and chug some water, the cold liquid soothing the scratchiness in my throat from screaming at Loraine. Once it stops feeling like sandpaper every time I swallow, I proceed to tell Jay everything that happened. Including showing him my broken phone. He is furious and I have to pull him back down to the couch when he says he wants to go over there. I would never let him do that. It will do no good and I just want to move on.

"Jay, just let it go. Please. I'm done. For good. I'm never going to go back there and I just want to put her and that place behind me. Please," I beg as I squeeze his hand and pull him closer to me on the couch.

"What about the rest of your stuff?" he asks.

"I have my school stuff and I was able to get one big load of clothes. The rest I don't need. In fact, I don't want it. I want all new things," I declare. I don't want anything that can even remotely remind me of that place.

"Okay. We'll get you all new things then," he agrees as he tucks a fallen strand of hair behind my ears.

I nod and he pulls me into him, wrapping me in his arms and my body relaxes for the first time all day, the throbbing in my head finally starting to fade. The combination of the Tylenol and Jay's arms around me are the perfect medicine.

"What about your birth certificate? Or Social? Do you have those things or know where they may be?"

"I have them. It's probably not smart, but as soon as I bought my car I took them from my mother's room and put them in the console. I didn't want her to have them and she never even noticed they were gone," I assure him.

"Good. I'll go get them and put them with my stuff, okay?"

I nod my head in agreement. "Thank you, Jay, for letting me stay here and for being here for me."

"Hey, look at me." He lifts my chin so that our eyes meet. "As much as I wish I had never been with Loraine, she led me to you. You're the best thing that's ever happened to me. Everything we went through was worth it to be here with you now. I want you to feel at home here. I don't want you to think of this as my apartment, it's our apartment now, okay? I love you."

I can barely manage words and all I am able to muster is, "I love you, Jay." And then I close the gap between our mouths so I can show him what I'm unable to tell him right now. He is being gentle and cautious with me, kissing me slowly and rubbing my back, but I want more right now, I *need* it. So, I climb on top of him, moving my lips faster against his, as I grind into him. He hardens under the pressure of my groin immediately, but he grabs my wrist and stops us.

"Emma, are you sure? I can't imagine what you're feeling right now."

"I need to feel you, Jay. That's all I need right now. Please. Please," I whimper, not even a little embarrassed at the desperation in my voice.

He stares at me, looking for something in my eyes that tells him I'm okay and that I really want this. "Please." It's pathetic, but I beg anyway.

Finally, he closes the gap between us and enhances our kiss. The numbness I felt earlier diminishes. The love I feel for this man consumes me and the fire in my core that burns when his lips are on mine makes me forget everything but the two of us.

I need him right here and right now, so my hands are on his belt, unbuckling it, and then moving to the buttons on his jeans. He is doing the same to mine. Our pants are off in a flash and I'm climbing back on top of him, my legs straddling his waist. He glides two fingers inside me and my head falls back with a groan. I grab his thickness with my hand and he pulls his fingers out of me so that I am able to glide down onto him, letting him fill me.

I move my body up and down, Jay's hands on my waist moving me with the perfect rhythm and it's not long until the waves of pleasure are flowing through us both. Our bodies connected, our moans conjoining and filling the apartment, and I never want it to end. I know at this moment that I want this with Jay for the rest of my life.

"You're it for me. I want this forever," I tell him, my voice trembling from the pleasure.

Jay's mouth meets mine again and he picks me up. My legs wrap around his waist and our bodies are still connected as he carries me to the bedroom.

He sits me on the bed and kisses the top of my head. "I'll be right back," he says to me as he takes off the last bit of clothing he has on.

He walks naked to the kitchen and then back into the bedroom to the bathroom and I take the opportunity to admire his toned body. I smile when I hear the bath running. I don't ever take baths because I don't have the time for them. Jay walks out of the bathroom and back over to me. He stands me up and pulls my shirt, the only article of clothing I still have on, over my head and then grabs my hand, guiding me into the bathroom.

"Wow," I say, shocked because the lights are dimmed, there are candles lit around the tub that is almost overflowing with bubbles.

"What can I say, I have a stressful job and baths are extremely relaxing." He laughs as he guides me in.

I sit down and the warm water against my tense muscles feels so good. Jay was right, it relaxes me instantly. He climbs in behind me and pulls me down into him, surrounding my body with his.

"Did you get off early?" I ask him, realizing it's only a little past three.

"No, when your phone went straight to voicemail, I cleared the rest of my afternoon and sped home. I was worried," he says as he squeezes me tighter into him.

"I'm sorry you had to do that," I apologize. I feel bad he had to cancel on patients because of me.

"Hey, don't be sorry! I love you and that's what people do when they're worried about their loved ones," he exclaims.

"I guess I'm not used to people worrying about me." It is a weird feeling, but I can't deny how nice it is.

"Well, get used to it," he says as he kisses the top of my head.

After we get out of the bath, Jay and I go to the store to get me a new phone. Luckily, I had insurance on mine to help cover some of the cost. He holds my hand while we're in the store, and wraps me in his arms multiple times as we wait for it to be ready.

It feels surreal to be in this moment with Jay right

now. For him to be making bubble baths for me and coming with me on simple errands. It seems like just yesterday, all we had were secret moments at a kitchen table.

# Chapter 23

As November continues to fly by, I try to focus all of my attention on Jay, school, and work. When I said I was done with Loraine, I meant it, but that last interaction with her took an intense toll on my body both mentally and physically and I am still trying to recover.

The other night while Jay and I were sitting at the kitchen table eating the fettuccine alfredo we made together, my new favorite pastime, he brought up the idea of me talking to a therapist. When I told him there was just no way I could afford that since the shop didn't offer insurance, he insisted he help and really didn't take no for an answer so I have my first appointment the Sunday after Thanksgiving. I would be lying if I said I wasn't nervous. I am aware that there is a lot of trauma that I have buried deep over the years, a lot of hurt and pain still nestled deep in the depths of my soul that I am not sure I am ready to pull to the surface. But as much as I want to be done with my mother and never have to think of her again, I know that if I want to move forward and really heal, this is something I have to do.

Thanksgiving is only a couple of days away and I find the thought a little nerve-wracking. This will be my first holiday spent with Jay and even though we live together, we have only been officially seeing each other for barely a month, so I feel weird bringing it up. What if he doesn't even intend to spend it with me? I am sure he has plans with his family.

I should have known better though because this morning as we eat our pancakes and drink our coffee, Jay casually asks, "What dessert should we bring to my mom's house tomorrow?" It isn't even a question if I'll be there. He says it as if we have had many thanksgivings together at his mom's house, and my heart swells at that, but I am also a bundle of nerves now. He has told me a lot about his relationship with his mom and brother and I know they are extremely close. Something I am unfamiliar with, but Jay is my life now. I want them to love me and I want to love them.

On top of that, I have never celebrated a holiday before in my life, *any* holiday. Not even Halloween. When I was little, I was sickeningly jealous of all the other kids when they would talk about their costumes and candy they got trick or treating and over time I just grew to hate the day and eventually I stopped caring about it all together, choosing to work or study on Halloween night instead of celebrating.

Thanksgiving and Christmas are the holidays that are the hardest for me. They were just ordinary days in my household growing up. In fact, Loraine didn't hesitate to tell me that Santa wasn't real the minute I was able to comprehend who Santa was. No turkey or pumpkin pie. No Christmas tree. No presents. No leaving out milk and cookies and snuggling on the couch waiting up for Santa. None of it.

That buzz of excitement that people feel around this time of year is a foreign concept to me. I have always impatiently waited for these end-of-year months to fly by because the, "what'd you get from Santa?" questions that filled the halls and classrooms after returning to school from winter break were always a punch to the gut. It wasn't the same as Halloween. Thanksgiving and Christmas are *family* holidays. And that sting of missing out hit deeper than missing out on candy. I would of course lie and through a forced smile tell everyone I got the popular Barbie doll or video game that everyone else was raving about.

It is not easy to go from dread to excitement after twenty-two years of the former, but I remind myself there is no need to feel that holiday angst anymore. I get to celebrate, *really* celebrate, this year and I can eat all the turkey and pumpkin pie that I want. I get to put up and decorate a Christmas tree for the first time in my life. Wrap presents and open them with Jay. I allow these thoughts in so they can fill the crevices of my mind, so they can push out all the negativity and I can allow myself to feel the joy that so many others get to feel this time of year.

I have a home now. A *real* home and it is time I start letting myself savor it. It is a weird thing, finally having a place to call home with someone that I love. This was not in the plan, and it definitely was not easy to get here, but I would not change one thing. Graduation is less than a month away now and even though I am not counting down to being out of that house anymore, I am just as ecstatic to walk across that stage knowing that it was me and me alone that got me there. That is an achievement that I earned all on my own and I am damn proud of myself for it.

# Chapter 24

Thursday morning is here before I know it and we are throwing our overnight bags in Jay's truck and hitting the road to his mom's house in Waco. We will be staying there tonight and then driving home in the morning. It is our first road trip together and even though Waco is only a few hours away, we go all out, stopping to get coffee and donuts on the way and we spend the drive learning even more about one another than we already have.

I learn that Jay is way more active than I knew. He tells me all about how he played tennis in high school and how he still enjoys playing the game a few times a month with some buddies of his. I learn that he runs on his lunch break and likes to go climbing on weekends. None of this surprises me, though. A person doesn't get Jay's toned physique by sitting on the couch playing video games.

He asks me about what my favorite hobbies are but then just seems sad for me when I tell him studying and making coffee, even though I say it as a joke. I tell him more about my childhood but then eventually decide to change the subject because I don't want that to dampen the mood and I can see the pity in Jay's eyes.

"You don't have to feel sorry for me," I tell him.

"I know, Emma, it's just not fair."

I take his hand and kiss it and then decide it is time for

some road trip games and we spend the last hour playing Would You Rather, which does a fantastic job at turning the mood around because it is impossible not to laugh when he asks, "Would you rather eat your own booger, or pick someone else's nose."

The three hours fly by and before I know it, we are pulling up to the cutest house I think I have ever seen. It is white, but not too white, it is more of a rustic white after years of weathering. There is brown trim around the windows and a bright yellow door that screams sunshine. A porch that wraps around the entire house and a white picket fence surrounds the property with two golden retrievers running around inside it, barking excitedly at the car as they run up and down the fence. The scene before me seems as if it is out of a movie and it is impossible not to smile at it.

"It's old, I know. But it's home." Jay pulls into the driveway and puts the car in park.

"It's perfect." It is the kind of home I have always envisioned having one day. A home I would spend with my husband and have babies in. The way that Jay was raised. It is the dream I have let myself fall asleep to for as long as I can remember. Quickly, I wipe away the tear that surprisingly rolls down my cheek, hoping Jay doesn't see it. But of course, he does.

"Hey… hey, what's wrong. Is this too much?" he asks and moves my hand to take over the tear-wiping job.

"No. Not at all. It's just. I've always had this dream of owning a house and raising a family and being the kind of mother that I always wanted and every time I've ever envisioned this, it's in a house very much like this one. It's just making me emotional, that's all."

He smiles and kisses me. "We're going to make that dream come true together, okay. I promise." And even though we have only known each other a short time, I believe him with every ounce of me.

We get out of the car and head to the trunk to grab our bags and I am trying desperately to hide my nerves at meeting his mom, although the bag that trembles in my hand is probably a dead giveaway. I realize that I have no idea how much she actually knows about me. A wave of terror washes over me as I realize that she may not even know *of* me.

"Wait!" I say frantically and grab his arm to stop him from heading any farther to the house. "Does she know I'm coming?" I ask frantically.

He chuckles and nods his head. "Of course, she knows you're coming, Emma."

I gulp and release a sigh of relief but then ask an even scarier question, "Does she know..." I pause, afraid to ask, and also afraid to hear the answer, but I *need* to know before I walk in that door so I force myself to ask, "Does she know how we met?"

He hesitates for a second. "Yes."

My eyes go wide, not expecting him to actually say yes, and I am sure I look a little crazy with my eyes bulging out of my head, but I am so mortified all of a sudden that I am this close to high-jacking his truck     and speeding out of here.

"My mom and I are close, and when she asked about

you and how we met, I didn't want to hide anything because I'm not ashamed about us. I love you and my mom is going to love you too, I promise. She was a little surprised when I told her, but she also didn't make it seem like a big deal. You're the first woman I've brought home in a long while so she knows how much you mean to me. And she's very excited to meet you."

His words calm me down just enough that I am able to take his hand when he reaches it out for me, and follow him up the wooden steps.

# Chapter 25

As we make our way through the house, my eyes sweep over every area and every piece of decoration I see. It does not look like anything has changed since Jay was probably just a boy. The couch is covered in floral fabric and all of the accent pieces are wooden and it is exactly what I imagined the inside of a country farmhouse to be. It is so incredibly warm and colorful and I swear I can actually feel the love that spreads deep into its walls, as if every happy Rowan family memory still lives within them.

Jay leads me straight to the kitchen where the smell of what I can only assume is Thanksgiving food fills the air, hitting my nostrils in the best way. The smell is divine and I have to swallow down the saliva that pools in my mouth.

Jay's mom is stuffing things inside a turkey when she turns around to see us, dropping the items in her hand and squealing as she runs over to Jay. I try to let go of his hand so he can properly embrace his mom, but he squeezes me tighter, refusing to release me, as he brings his mom in for a tight one-armed hug. She holds on to him tight, squeezing him and repeating "oh my Jay!" over and over and it is an adorable sight that makes all the nerves I was feeling disappear. She lets go of him after what feels like a good five minutes and immediately turns to face me with an ear to ear grin that is so welcoming it is impossible not to return.

"Mom, this is Emma; Emma, this is my mom, Ruth." His mom barely gives him time to finish the introduction before bringing me in for a hug. This time, Jay does let go of my hand so that I am able to hug Ruth back. And although physical affection is not something that I am used to, it is an easy thing to do with Ruth. The feeling of being embraced, by a mom, especially by *Jay's* mom, makes me feel as if I can do anything. As if I am loved and supported and I let myself relish in it.

"It is so nice to meet you, Emma." She holds my hands in hers and I don't think I ever want her to let them go.

"You too, Mrs. Rowan." I know Jay introduced her as Ruth, but I don't have a lot of experience meeting people's parents. Well, none really. And I want to be polite.

"Oh, call me Ruth, sweetie!" She encourages me, and I smile and say okay.

"Where's Robert?" Jay asks, talking about his brother. From what I have learned about Robert, he is more of a free spirit who likes to do odd jobs here and there instead of settling down in one career. He is a couple years younger than Jay, making him twenty-six.

"He should be here any minute," Ruth answers as she goes back to working on the turkey.

"Come on, I'll show you around!" Jay grabs my hand and tells his mom we'll be back.

He gives me a full tour of the adorable three-bedroom, two-bath farmhouse that he grew up in, the coziness from downstairs continues through every inch of every room.

We put our bags in his childhood room that we will be sleeping in later, making me grateful that his mom doesn't seem to mind us sharing a room, and then walk outside to go see the farm.

"Hello, my sweet girls!" he says to the two golden retrievers I saw earlier as he kneels down, letting them jump all over him and kiss all over his face. They turn to me now and I flinch a little as they beg for my attention because even though I yearned for one as a girl, I am not used to being around the furry creatures. It only takes a second of them loving on me though and I am on the floor with them soaking up their affection.

Jay's looking down on us laughing and admiring my moment with the dogs. "I've never really been around dogs. Or any animals really," I confess.

He kisses me on the forehead. "That'll definitely change by the time we leave here tomorrow morning." He chuckles.

We walk into the barn and I am immediately greeted by a strong smell of hay, and what I guess is normal farm life. They don't have a ton of animals, but he introduces me to their three donkeys, two goats, two pigs, and multiple chickens.

He tells me all about their farm chores they did growing up and how his mom does such a good job taking care of them all on her own now. "She is a retired teacher so she loves it because it keeps her busy," he tells me. I am not sure farm life is for me, but I love being out here with them right now, learning all about the way Jay grew up and giving me more of a glimpse into his childhood.

We head back inside and are greeted by Robert's presence when we enter the kitchen again. Robert is louder than Jay and very outgoing, which has always been a quality in other people that intimidated me, but he is surprisingly very easy to talk to. Jay's free-spirited description of him is spot on. His style is less polished than Jay, and more grunge, but it works for him. His hair is brown like Jay's but longer and messy, like he hasn't brushed it in a while, but like the grunge attire, it also works for him. The messy hair is paired with a beard and his whole look, although not my type, looks good on him. He lives in a van, that he converted, full time and travels around the country. I can't help but think about how well he and Jessica would hit it off.

I offer to help Ruth with the rest of the food, and she puts me in charge of the green bean casserole. I may not know a lot about thanksgiving food, but I do know my way around the kitchen, so she only needs to tell me the instructions once and I am able to throw the dish together easily.

Jay and Robert are watching football in the living room and I can hear them catching up over the whistles and cheers from the TV. The dogs, now inside the house, run around the kitchen, their paws pitter pattering across the hardwood. Ruth hums as she opens up the oven to check on the Turkey, the strong smell of flavors wafting out and filling the air. For a brief moment, I stop what I am doing, unable to stir the casserole as I get stuck in a moment of gratitude. Frozen in place at the shock of the experience. If you would have asked me three months ago if this is where I thought I would be right now, I would have laughed in your face. It feels like a dream to be standing here right now. To be spending Thanksgiving Day with Jay and his family. To be welcomed. To feel love and warmth, instead of hatred and callousness. It is so easy to forget about my old life with Loraine on a day like this.

We all sit down to eat around two p.m. and I have to physically control myself at the dinner table because I have never had food this good. The conversation is lovely, and it flows easily. Ruth never brings up what she knows about how Jay and I met and for that I am thankful. I am not sure if Robert knows, but he never once asks how we got together, which tells me he might.

"Mmmm, Emma, I know this green bean casserole is my recipe, but I don't think it's ever tasted this good!" Ruth says from across the table.

"She's been cooking for herself for quite some time and every dish she makes is delicious," Jay chimes in and leans over to kiss me on the cheek. I blush.

I am nervous for a second that one of them might ask more about that, and I will have to dive into my childhood, but to my relief, they don't.

"Thank you. But really, it's the turkey and stuffing that are incredible, Ruth. Thank you so much for having me."

"Oh, sweetie, we are so glad you're here." She grabs my hand from across the table and gives me the most genuine smile.

"That's great and all, but what about my cranberries?" Robert jokes and we all laugh because we watched him open the can of cranberries he must have grabbed on the drive over and pour them on to a plate.

Somehow, we find more room to stuff our faces with the pumpkin pie I made last night and Ruth praises my cooking even more. I smile as I envision us cooking and celebrating together in this kitchen for years to come.

The boys clean up the kitchen while Ruth and I relax with a glass of wine and chat some more and then we spend the rest of the night drinking more wine and playing thirty-one. By the time ten p.m. rolls around, we are all exhausted and ready for bed. Robert sleeps in his van which I find so interesting, but he says it's where he feels most comfortable.

Jay and I find sleep only after we've christened the room he grew up in. My cheeks are flush afterward, not only from the orgasm I just had but from the thought of Jay's mom having heard us.

"There's no way," Jay assures me. "Her room is downstairs and we were quiet." We both laugh at that. "We were *kind of* quiet," he corrects himself.

I fall asleep in a state of contentment that I have never truly felt before. My heart is so full and when we say goodbye to Ruth the next morning, I am genuinely sad and I know that even though I just met her, I am going to miss her until I see her again. She promises to come to my graduation and even though I insist that is not necessary, she promises me she will be there, and I hug her tightly before we climb in the car and head home. I close my eyes as we pull out of the driveway and soak in the feeling of having a home that I am happy to go home to.

# Chapter 26

It is Sunday morning and the high from my first Thanksgiving is wearing off, leaving me with an unease I can't quite place, but feel as it settles deep down in the pit of my stomach. I have no idea why because all I feel is happiness. But it feels as if I am *too* happy. As if life is *too* perfect right now. Anxiety is trying to fight the joy that has made home in my heart these past few weeks. It feels as if a shoe is gonna drop soon. Like there is no possible way I can feel this happy. No possible way that my life from just half a year ago could have turned into this beautiful thing it is now. Although I have moved on, Loraine still lingers in the back of my mind. I want nothing to do with her anymore, but I can't help the feeling that she is going to try and mess things up. That there is no way that after years of torment from her, she is just going to let me be happy. Especially when, in her eyes, I have stolen her boyfriend.

On top of all of this, I have my first therapy appointment this afternoon and the nerves are already kicking in, making my heart jolt out of my chest every time I think about it. My mind won't stop racing, thinking about all of the things that she may ask me about Loraine or my childhood and for a quick second, right as I am about to head out the door, I think about canceling. But Jay swoops in and gives me the encouragement that I need to get in my car and head to her office.

Her name is Claire and the minute I sit down with her, my nerves quiet down a bit because I can tell instantly that she radiates a warmth a lot like Ruth's. She does not dig into anything too tough today which I am thankful for. Instead, she asks me simple questions about myself like what my parents do, thankfully she doesn't ask any more questions after I say I don't know who my father is and my mom is an unemployed alcoholic. She just nods her head, tells me that it must be difficult and continues on. She asks if I have any siblings, any friends, where I go to school and what I want to do after I graduate.

Before I know it, the hour is already up, and it was a whole lot less scary than I thought it would be. We didn't dive into anything too traumatic; instead, Claire kept it surface level, sticking with the basic, factual questions about myself. It was like dipping your toes into the pool instead of taking the plunge right in.

I head to the coffee shop right after my appointment for the night shift with Jessica. I had not told her yet about me starting therapy and she is, of course, ecstatic for me the minute I tell her where I just came from. Making me feel even better about my decision to start. She tells me all about her Thanksgiving back home in Austin and I fill her in on my Thanksgiving with Jay's family. I even include how I think she would be a perfect match for Robert. She is practically drooling when I tell her that he has a beard and lives full time in a van, traveling the country.

My time here at the coffee shop with Jessica is coming to an end with graduation right around the corner. I have already started applying to some entry-level marketing positions around Houston. Snaps Coffee Joint has never been anything but good to me and I really do love making coffee, but I am excited for this next step. Not working with Jessica is really going to suck though. I know I will still see her, but it won't be near as much, so I really want to soak up this time with her. We spend our shift, and all the other shifts throughout the week, remembering our most fun moments working together and we even start to plan some hang outs outside of work.

The next week zooms by. I spend every waking moment studying or working and Jay has to basically force me into bed every night at three a.m. But before I know it, I am turning in my last final and walking off campus for the last time until graduation.

I soak in all the views and smells of campus as I walk to my car. I cannot believe I am here. I have dreamt of this moment for so long now. To top it off, I get to go home and celebrate with Jay tonight. I cannot believe this is my life now. But the moment that thought flickers in my mind, all the excitement I had just felt seems to get smothered. There it is again. That anxiety and doubt I felt earlier this week creeps back in, trying to suffocate my happiness. I push it down, unwilling to let it ruin this moment, and walk off campus for the last time until I am walking across the stage.

# Chapter 27

It's a totally new feeling being able to enjoy your free time without the lingering worry of assignments and tests. But unfortunately, it seems I didn't get much of a break without something to consume my thoughts. We are relaxing on the couch, Jay on one end while I am on the other, my feet in his lap, his hands massaging every inch of them. The first time it dings, I can see the tension spread over his face when he looks at it. He doesn't respond though, only sets it down next to him where it had previously been. Five minutes later, it goes off again. This time, he looks annoyed and I watch as he finally responds to whoever it is. Before he sets his phone back down, I see him silence it and my heart plummets.

The feeling of anxiety that I had been shoving down these past couple weeks is coursing through me now, taking over. Something is going on. I can feel it. Something capable of popping this joyous bubble I have been living in.

"Everything okay?" I ask, trying to keep my voice steady and calm.

He hesitates for one second, not even a second, and it is such a small hesitation he probably doesn't even think I noticed anything. But I did. "Yep. Everything's good, just work."

But I can tell he is lying. On top of that, it's Sunday, his office is closed. I squeeze my hands together tightly, so tight in fact that it feels as if I'm going to rupture skin with my nails, but it's the only thing I can do to get my nerves to settle, to keep my hands from shaking.

I knew that something was going on. That something was going to try and steal all of this away from me. I was too happy and I should have known this life I had found with Jay couldn't be found *that* easily. Jay doesn't grab his phone again, but I know he is still getting messages. As I pretend to be watching the movie we have on, I can see him out of the corner of my eye glancing down at his phone every few minutes at what I assume are more texts coming in. But from who? Who would he be getting texts from that would make him want to lie? To keep a secret from me? The lingering anxiety was spilling over now, making my blood run thick, making my head, neck, fingers, limbs, *everything* on me pulse heavy.

Jay was off as we got ready for bed that night. Again, doing everything he could to seem normal. He hugged me from behind while I was brushing my teeth, rubbed his hand up and down my arm as he lay next to me in bed. Kissed my temple and then my mouth before saying goodnight and rolling over, but I could see it in his eyes. Something was off. I wanted to check his phone, to see who it was that had texted him, but I didn't want to be *that* girl. And besides, I don't know his passcode.

Sleep fought me all night just as the anxiety had been fighting my joy all week. When I wake at eight a.m. after only having fallen asleep at five, my heart stops when I notice Jay is not in bed with me and when I check my phone, I feel sick when I read a text from him. *"Had to head to the office for an emergency, see you after your shift. Love you."*

It was not like Jay to leave without saying bye; even if I was asleep, he would kiss me and rub my hair enough to wake me up at least slightly. But nothing. At least I don't think so. I was probably passed out from exhaustion when he left, but I know I would have woken up if he had kissed me. My body responded too strongly to his touch, I would have woken up, I know it.

I tried to keep my mind off of whatever was going on with Jay as I spent the morning researching and preparing for the interviews I have on Thursday. My shift at the coffee shop started at ten and I was thankful to have the distraction, but it's now two in the afternoon and I have only heard from Jay once and that was just in response to me asking if chicken noodle soup was okay for dinner. The lack of communication is making it hard to focus but thankfully, Jessica is also working today and I am able to unload some of my worries onto her.

"Maybe there's a lot of sick animals right now and he's just extra busy and maybe last night, he really *was* getting texts from work," she says, trying to ease my worries. But it doesn't work. I know Jay better than I have ever known anyone and I know deep down that he is keeping something from me.

Our shift ends at five and I am thankful for the busy

after-work crowd to help make these last thirty minutes fly by so I can get home to Jay and ask him to be honest about what is going on. I am making a vanilla latte when my phone chimes. I don't typically get out my phone when I am making someone's drink, but I am too anxious to see if it's Jay. But when my screen comes into view and I see who it's from, everything around me turns into a blur and the only thing I can hear is the pounding in my ears.

Loraine.

In my almost twenty-two years of life, well, since I have had a phone, Loraine has never texted me. Not *once*. And I know before I even open the text that it was her who was texting Jay last night. I can feel it in my bones.

That doesn't stop the paper cup filled with hot coffee from falling out of my hands and landing on the floor, scalding coffee hitting my ankles, as I read the message from my mother.

*"Can you tell Jay that he left his wallet at breakfast? Thanks hun."* Above it is a picture of Jay's black leather wallet.

I am frozen. Unable to move. Or breathe. Or see straight.

"Emma? Emma, what's wrong?" I can hear Jessica, I can even feel her hands on my arms, but I am unable to respond. Unable to use my voice. All I can do is hand her my phone so she can see the text from Loraine.

"Oh my god," she whispers.

"Um, hello? Is that my coffee that's on the ground?" a man asks, the irritation in his voice seems a million miles away instead of the two feet it really is. I can hear Jessica apologize to him and tell him she will have it ready in just a minute before turning back to me. "Go sit down, Emma, our shift is practically over, I'll finish up."

I don't respond, but I guess my body is following her instructions because after a few minutes, I am sitting in a comfy leather chair, trying to breathe back some life inside of me and figure out what the hell is going on. Jay went to breakfast with Loraine? He has been texting her? My mind starts going to all the darkest places. What if they never stopped talking? What if he has still been seeing her?

My mind seems to know better though. I feel betrayed right now, but I know Jay. I know he wouldn't still be seeing Loraine. I know he never loved her and I know he hates her just as much as I do for everything she's put him through. But *why?* Why would he go see her?

She must have something over him. She has to. That is the only explanation. But either way, I am devastated. She was supposed to be out of our lives for good. I was supposed to be done with her. Jay getting fucking breakfast with her and, on top of that, *keeping* it from me was doing the exact opposite. I realize when the shock wears off how fucking angry I am. Furious. Furious with Jay for doing this behind my back, whatever the reason, and making me look like an idiot.

"Hey." Jessica sits down cautiously across from me. "You okay?" she asks.

"I'm angry," I say.

"As you fucking should be!" she exclaims.

"I don't want to see him right now," I tell her.

"I don't blame you. Come on, stay with me tonight.

We'll get wine and ice cream and drink and eat 'til you feel better."

I love her and once again I have never been more grateful to have a friend like her at a time like this. She is my best friend and when she reaches her hand out for me, I take it without hesitation.

# Chapter 28

Jay has called me five times in the past hour, despite me texting him saying I was staying at Jessica's tonight. I didn't tell him I knew about his breakfast date with my mother.

"You don't really think anything happened, right? I mean, it was totally shitty meeting up with her, but it's obvious he loves you," she says and I sigh because I know she's right. I know he loves me and I know there has to be a reasonable explanation for this and that is making ignoring these phone calls extremely difficult.

"No, I know Jay wouldn't do that, it's the fact that he kept it a secret, even when I specifically asked him last night if everything was okay. And him keeping it from me gave Loraine exactly what she wanted. The ability to humiliate me."

"Yah, I'm really not sure what Jay was thinking. It's all totally fucked up for sure," she agrees as she takes a sip of her wine before adding, "but if I could take a guess, I would assume that he thought he was doing the right thing. That keeping it from you was protecting you. I'm not saying that he was right in doing that, just trying to give you another perspective."

My phone rings again just as Jessica finishes talking and I pick up because I know she's right, because I know that even though what he did was wrong, he thought meeting with Loraine was the right thing to do. I have no idea why he did it, but I do trust that he did it for the right reasons.

"Hello?" I answer.

"Emma, thank god." He lets out a breath it seems he's been holding all day.

"Where are you?" he asks even though I have already told him where I am.

"Jessica's."

"Why? It's almost nine o'clock. What is going on?"

"Where's your wallet?" I ask.

"Huh?"

"Your wallet. Where is it?"

"Um, I don't know," he answers and I can hear him as he starts looking around for it. "Damn, I must have left it at work."

"Wrong," I reply.

"Emma. Please fucking tell me what is happening."

"Your wallet isn't at work." Silence rings though the phone so I continue. "Loraine has it. You left it at y'alls little breakfast date this morning," I say, sounding as casual and chipper as I possibly can.

"Fuck. Jessica, I can explain. It's not what you think. *Please* come home so we can talk."

"Oh, I don't think it was anything. I know you wouldn't do that," I assure him and I can hear him breathe out another sigh of relief.

"So why are you there? Why won't you come home?"

"Because you lied to me, Jay. I know it was her who

was texting you last night and I asked you specifically if something was wrong and you lied straight to my face and then you left this morning without as much as a goodbye so that you could meet up with *her* and then you avoid me all day. That is why I am fucking mad, Jay."

"Emma." His voice is pleading. "There is a reason I didn't tell you. Will you please come home so I can explain everything? I love you."

The desperation in the way he says "I love you" has me almost running out the door straight into his arms, but then I remember the anger and humiliation I felt when I opened Loraine's text and it's easy to stop myself.

"I love you too, Jay. But I'm hurt and embarrassed and you lied to me. I'm not ready to come home yet. I'm going to stay here at Jessica's tonight."

"Okay." He sighs, giving in, knowing he won't be able to convince me otherwise.

"I love you, Emma. I was trying to protect you from her," he tells me again.

I sigh because I know deep down that is the truth, but it doesn't take away the pain and hurt I'm feeling. "I love you too Jay, but I've been protecting myself from her my whole life, what I need from you is honesty" I say and then hang up.

Jessica and I spend the night watching silly rom coms and eating ice cream until we are sick to our stomachs. It feels almost childish, as if we are in middle school having a sleepover and I realize this is something I needed way more than I ever realized. It's as if something inside me is being healed. My inner child that longed for friendships is finally getting the love that she's always needed.

We drink wine and I tell Jessica about the interviews I have coming up and how Jay and I are talking about moving into a new place so we can start fresh, which despite everything I am still excited about. Jessica tells me about her plan to travel for six months after she graduates in May and I think to myself again how well she and Robert would get along so I tell her more about him and she swoons and begs me to introduce them as soon as possible.

"I am so over college boys," she states.

"We'll have to set up a double date soon!" I exclaim and she squeals at the thought of it.

Later that night as I lie next to Jessica, who snores apparently, I feel an immense amount of desire to be lying next to Jay instead. My mind wanders to everything we have been through these past few months. I think about the first time I saw him, how I felt an undeniable connection to him. How that connection never seemed to falter even through months of uncertainty. I think about all of our secret moments we shared in the kitchen. All of our after-hour chats. How it felt the first time he touched me, our first kiss, the night at his apartment after he had saved me from what could have been the worst night of my life. In every single one of those moments, I fell in love with him more and more, despite him being with my mother.

I have never loved anyone in my entire life until I met Jay and I know without question that I will love him for the rest of it. I know that after everything we have been through, there is nothing that could tear us apart, especially not Loraine. And as if I've been woken up for the first time in the past twelve hours, I realize that by being away from Jay right now I am letting her win. I am giving her exactly what she wants and it isn't Jay I should be angry at, it's her. It will always be her. And with that, I grab my phone from the nightstand next to me, find Loraine's number, block her, and then delete her from my life once and for all. I feel an immense weight lifted from my shoulders.

Unable to be away from Jay another minute, I get up, grab my things and head home. To Jay. Because anywhere that Jay is, is where I want to be. For the rest of my life. I shoot Jessica a text when I make it into our apartment, just letting her know that I had come home so she didn't worry when she woke up and then I quietly sneak into our bedroom.

Jay is asleep, looking absolutely peaceful and perfect, and I know that I can't be mad at him anymore. That I need him. Now. And I want to show him that no matter what, we will always be okay. That I will always love him.

I slip off my clothes so that I'm completely naked and climb into our bed and wrap myself around him. He squirms a bit when my body makes contact with him and when I press my lips to his neck, he finally opens his eyes just enough to see me.

"Baby," he whispers. "You came home."

"I missed you," I say as I climb on top of him and when his hands roam over my body and he finds that I'm completely unclothed, he groans and pulls me down to him to meet his lips to mine.

My lips fold around his, our bare chests pressing

together and when he grabs my waist and pulls me to grind over him, I can feel him through his boxers already ready for me.

"God, I love you," he moans into my ear as I roll my hips over him again.

"I love you, too. So much."

He stops my hips from grinding over him again before he says, "We should talk, Emma. I want to explain."

I want him to explain, I do. I want to know what he was thinking and why he thought going to breakfast with my mother behind my back was a good idea, but I want this more. I *need* this more.

"Not now. Tomorrow," I tell him as I ignore his attempt to stop me and push my hips harder into him, rubbing my bare self over the hard bulge under his boxers. He hisses in my ear and bites my neck as I rub over him again, soaking his boxers with my wetness.

"I need you," I pant and with that, Jay flips me over so that his warm body is pressed on top of me and he shoves two fingers deep inside me, hitting the spot only he knows how to, and I cry out.

"God, you are wet," he says right before his mouth makes contact with my nipple. He bites it gently between his teeth and I writhe under him. Beg him for more. His lips trail down, his tongue making a trail all the way until his mouth hovers over my wetness, his fingers still thrusting in and out of me.

"Please," I beg and that's all it takes. His tongue sweeps over my flesh that's throbbing for him. I scream at the contact and he doesn't stop. Not 'til I feel the waves of pleasure building with each contact of his tongue on me.

"God, you taste so good," he says as his mouth meets mine again. I can still taste myself on him and it adds a whole new wave of desire. I grab hold of him, hard and ready, and pull him towards my entrance that's still soaking for him. Still ready for him even after the orgasm he just gave me. He thrusts inside of me. Over and over until I'm once again crying out, screaming his name.

He holds me after, planting kisses all over my face. Telling me he loves me over and over and I relish in it.

"Do you want to talk?" he asks and I shake my head no. This moment is too perfect, too sweet, and I don't want to ruin it. I want to enjoy it, soak it in. Be fully present in it. With him.

"Tomorrow," I tell him.

"Okay. Tomorrow," he agrees and pulls me in tighter so that there is no space between us and that's where I stay the rest of the night.

# Chapter 29

The next morning, I wake to an empty bed and my heart sinks. But only for a second because as soon as I breathe in, I can smell the coffee and bacon wafting in our room from the kitchen. I throw the covers off me and pull my robe on.

"Hey," Jay says when he sees me walk into the kitchen. "Go get back in bed, I was just about to bring you breakfast," he states.

I smile, kiss him, and then head back to the room and cozy up back underneath the sheets. I check my phone and see two texts from Jessica. The first letting me know she's glad I made it home safely. And the second reads, *"I can't believe tomorrow is our last day at the shop together!"* Followed by about ten sad face emojis. My heart sinks. In all of the drama of these past couple of days, I had completely forgotten tomorrow was our last day working together. Jay convinced me to quit even though I don't have a job yet. He said I deserved some time off after a very grueling few years and honestly, he's right. I have some money saved up, and hopefully with the interviews I have scheduled, I will have a new job soon. But not getting to see Jessica multiple times a week is already making me sad.

Jay comes in holding a tray and that instantly makes

me feel better. He sets the tray down in front of me and on it is a cup of coffee with cream, the perfect shade of caramel, just the way I like it, a stack of pancakes, and a pile of bacon. It smells heavenly.

"You didn't have to do this," I tell him, although I am very glad he did because I'm already shoving a bite of pancake in my mouth and it's delicious.

"I know, but I wanted to."

"Can I explain myself now?" he asks and I nod yes, unable to talk with a mouthful of bacon.

"Loraine texted me Sunday night asking for details about your graduation. She seemed genuinely interested in being there, but I was very hesitant to tell her anything so when she asked to grab breakfast to hear more about the details of your graduation, I felt like it was a good idea so that I could look her in the eye and truly gauge her. See if she really was interested in coming." He stopped and rubbed his forehead with his hands before continuing. "I could tell immediately that she was full of it. She was flirting with me from the second I walked in and didn't ask one thing about you for a good five minutes. When I brought up your graduation, she changed the subject and I could tell she was playing some sort of a game, so I told her that breakfast was over and that she needed to leave the both of us alone and then left. I was there for twenty minutes tops, but I guess I left my wallet on the table. Or now that I think about it, she probably swiped it when I went to ask the waiter for the check. Anyway, I debated all day on whether or not I should tell you. She's already hurt you so much I didn't want to add to any more of the pain she's caused. But I should have realized when she didn't ask any questions about your graduation, despite that being why she wanted to meet up, that she had a plan. I'm so sorry, Emma. I should have told you on Sunday, the second that she texted me. I fucked up."

He rests his forehead on mine as he whispers another sorry and I have no anger or hurt in me towards him anymore. Only love and gratitude.

"I should have known from the start that you were doing what you thought was right, Jay. I should have realized immediately that it was Loraine and only Loraine doing the wrong thing. Trying to hurt us and pull us apart, but I'm not going to let that happen. I'm not going to let her have any effect on my life anymore. On *our* lives."

"Good." He breathes out a sigh of relief as he kisses me.

"I blocked her. And deleted her from my phone. I am done."

"I'll do the same." And he does. He takes out his phone right then and there, blocks her number and then deletes her.

It's an automatic relief knowing she is *officially* out of our lives for good and I feel a new lightness, that dooming feeling of anxiety I had been feeling no longer exists and it feels good. I make a bite of pancakes with my fork and feed it to Jay, then he kisses me again, and I laugh when he starts rubbing his mouth over mine, leaving sweet sticky syrup all over my lips.

Jay heads off to work and since I had work yesterday during my normally scheduled therapy session, we moved it to this morning. She starts off by asking how I am and instead of skirting around it, I dive in and tell her everything that has happened this weekend. Which means, I also have to tell her a little bit more about my mother and how I am dating her ex-boyfriend. She doesn't once judge me, instead she just listens and lets me get it all out and when I'm done, I can't believe how good I feel.

"Wow, it sounds like you have had quite the rollercoaster of a few months," she says.

"My emotions have never been so all over the place. I have cried, both good and bad tears, more than I ever have in my whole life. In fact, I don't think I cried for probably ten years before all this started. It felt like I was going crazy."

"Tell me, Emma, why do you think you didn't cry for so long?" she asks.

"Oh. I don't know. I think with the way I grew up it was easier to just be numb."

"So, maybe you didn't go crazy, maybe you're just letting yourself feel for the first time in a very long time."

Her words hit me like a brick. All these months I thought I was losing it. All the tears, all the anger. But I wasn't losing it. I was just having emotions for the first time in years and instead of feeling embarrassed by them, I feel proud of myself.

# Chapter 30

Twenty-two. I wake up Tuesday morning feeling refreshed and ecstatic to be starting a new year at the same time as I'm starting this whole new life with Jay and for once, I am actually excited for my birthday. I'm spending the first half working my last shift with Jessica and then this evening, Jay is taking me out. He won't tell me any details and I am giddy with excitement.

When I show up to work, Jessica squeals and hugs me. "Happy Birthday!"

"Thank you!" I laugh and hug her back.

"It's weird. I'm happy to spend part of your birthday with you, but I'm also so sad this is our last work day together. I can't believe it."

"I know it feels so weird. So many new things are happening," I say.

"Good things!" she adds.

"Yes, very good things!" I agree.

"Here," she says as she hands me the gift bag she had been holding.

"You didn't have to do this!" I say as I open the bag. I pull out a coffee mug that has a picture of Jessica and me on it. A selfie we took last year on a slow day. We had just made ourselves coffees and were enjoying the down time. I hold it to my chest and feel the tears start to sting my eyes, but I don't try to stop them or get annoyed that I'm crying again. Instead, I let myself feel the emotions. To feel how good it is to have a friend like Jessica.

"Thank you so much!" I say through the lump in my throat and then pull her into an embrace.

"Of course. I love you, Emma! You're my best friend," she says as she starts to get choked up too.

An awkward cough at the register breaks the sweet moment and we both apologize as we wipe our tears.

"Last day," I say, explaining the tears.

"Ahhh gotcha," he says and then pulls a twenty dollar bill out and drops it into the tip jar.

The shift comes and goes and before I know it, we're hugging and crying again in the parking lot before we part ways after a shift for the last time.

I get home before Jay and get ready for our date tonight. I still don't know where we are going, but he says it's nice so I wear a mid-thigh length button down black dress with yellow, pink and orange flowers all over it. I pair it with black heels and pull my hair back into a high pony.

When Jay walks into the door at five-thirty, he's holding a bouquet of roses and I melt.

"Happy Birthday, baby," he says as he hands them to me and pulls me in for a long kiss. I moan into him and he pulls away. I frown playfully.

He laughs. "We have a reservation to make!"

"Okay, okay," I say.

"I'm going to go shower really fast and change, get those in some water? I don't have any vases, but I do have a large glass in one of these cabinets."

I rummage through the cabinets until I find the glass that I assume he was talking about. It's just a large drinking glass and I laugh to myself. *Men.*

Jay comes out in fitted black slacks and a stripe-patterned button down. He looks glorious.

"Ready?" he asks as he reaches his hand out for me.

"Ready!"

After driving for about five minutes, I start getting a little confused because I had assumed we would stay in the city for dinner. Instead, we seem to be leaving it.

"Where are we goinggg?" I beg him to tell me.

"It's a surprise!"

"Ughhh."

After another five minutes, we are driving in an area called The Heights. I love this area because the houses are adorable and feel so homey but are still so close to the city.

My confusion grows even more when we slow in front of a cute white house with black rimmed windows and an adorable yellow door that reminds me of his mom's house. Jay motions for me to get out so I do, and he follows. I'm trying to think of anyone who may live here, but I, of course, can't because besides Jay and Jessica, I am not close to anyone else in Houston.

But then I see it. The "For Sale" sign.

"What is this?" I ask as I turn to see him standing behind me with an enormous grin on his face.

"Hopefully our new house," he says so simply, like it isn't the greatest news on Earth.

"What?" I say, shock etched in my voice. I turn back

to stare at the gorgeous home.

"It's not official," he says as he makes his way closer to me, wrapping his arms around me. "But I put in an offer this morning. And my realtor thinks they'll accept."

I'm speechless. I can't believe this. This is the house of my dreams.

"Are you mad I didn't tell you? I wanted it to be a surprise. I was going to wait 'til they accepted, but I wanted to make sure that this is something you want too. That you love it as much as I do."

"Are you kidding? It's perfect. I love it. I love you. So much," I say as I turn around and jump into his arms.

"I love you too, baby," he says before he brings our mouths together.

When we get to the restaurant and I see we're eating at "Vic & Anthony's Steakhouse," I can't help but laugh.

"Is this the steak dinner you got at the auction?" I ask. The dinner I stupidly thought he was trying to get for Loraine. That feels like a lifetime ago.

"Yes." He smiles. "The plan was always to bring you here."

I smile at how far we've come in such a short period of time. We spend the dinner looking at photos of the inside of what is hopefully our new home and then we go home and spend the rest of the evening in bed. It's the best birthday of my life.

# Chapter 31

The next evening, we're in the kitchen cooking our favorite meal, Fettuccine Alfredo with chicken, when Jay's phone rings.

"Hey, John!" Jay says as he answers the call and I turn to look at him, knowing that John is his realtor and he must be calling about the house.

Jay's face lights up at whatever it is John is saying to him and he pulls me into him.

"Awesome! Thanks so much, John!" he says and then hangs up.

"You ready to make a home with me?" he asks, his voice deep and sexy, but excited at the same time.

"God, YES." I squeal.

"They accepted our offer and we should be closing on it in a month," he says and I squeal again.

I love this apartment with Jay, I really do. It is the first place I ever felt at home, the place where our relationship became real, and I do feel some sadness when I think about leaving it. But at the same time, there are still lingering memories here of a harder time. Like when I was drugged or when I wanted Jay so badly but couldn't have him. And even knowing that Loraine spent time here at the beginning of their relationship is hard to stomach sometimes. I'm ready to start somewhere new with the love of my life.

He kisses me and even though I can hear the chicken sizzling, telling me it needs to be flipped, it's impossible not to enhance it. He picks me up and sits me on the counter, my legs spread for him as he moves to stand in between them and I wrap them around his waist. He groans when I part his lips with my tongue and then when I bite his lower lip gently with my teeth, he squeezes my hips, pulling me against his groin to feel him hard beneath me. I whimper and pull him even closer, running my tongue over his lip.

His hands move fast to pull down my shorts and before I even have the chance to work at getting his sweatpants down, his fingers push aside the small piece of fabric of my panties and he thrusts two fingers inside of me. I cry out and push my hips into him so that his fingers hit just the right spot. His mouth moves to my neck, kissing, biting, and licking and just as I am about to beg him to be inside me, I remember the chicken.

"The chicken!" I scream and we both turn to see smoke floating above the chicken that is very clearly burning. Jay reaches to turn the stove top off with his free hand, his other still buried deep inside me, his fingers continuing to pump in and out of me. Never stopping their glorious movement.

"Please, Jay," I whine. "I need you…" – it's hard to concentrate with the pressure that is building inside me from the spot his fingers hit over and over. I really do not want him to stop, but I need more than his fingers – "inside me," I finally manage to get out.

Jay pulls his fingers from me and I whimper at the loss of them even though I know what is coming is a million times better. I help him pull down his pants and then free his length from his boxers and in no time at all, I can feel the tip of him right at my entrance. My panties are still pushed to the side, neither of us bothering to remove them. He rubs just the head of him slowly up and down my slit, torturing me.

My eyes close and my head flies back as I plead with him some more to close the space between us completely, but instead, he grabs my face with his free hand, pulling me to look at him.

"I fucking love you," he says right as he plunges into me.

# Chapter 32

It's Friday night. The night before my graduation. Jay's mom is here and we're cooking dinner together in the kitchen while Jay showers after his day at the clinic. Even though she told me she would be at my graduation, it still feels so surreal. Just six months ago, I didn't think anyone, except maybe Jessica, but certainly not my mother, would be watching me walk across the stage to get my diploma. Now, not only will the love of my life be there, but also this warm, motherly figure that has come into my life right along with him.

"I know you're the only girlfriend of his I've ever met, but I can tell that you're the one for him, Emma. The love I see in his eyes when he looks at you..." She has to stop for a moment and I can see the tears swelling in her eyes. She continues, "It's the same way his father looked at me." She wipes a tear from her cheek and I hug her tight.

"I love your son so much. He's the best thing that has ever happened to me," I say into her ear and she tightens our hug even more.

Over dinner, I get to hear more about Jay's childhood and the farm. All about the different times he helped his dad with the animals and the moment that Ruth knew he would work with animals one day. There was an evening when Jay was fifteen that a stray dog had taken shelter in their barn one night when a vicious thunderstorm had blown over town. They found the dog the next morning when the storm finally blew over and they realized quickly that she was pregnant. And scared. So scared that she seemed extremely aggressive and after a few hours of them talking to her, and trying to reassure her, it was Jay that was able to earn her trust. The story is beautiful and I'm not the least bit surprised by it. Of course, he was.

In the blink of an eye, it's Saturday morning, *graduation* morning, and I'm waking to Jay covering my face in kisses and I'm not sure there is a better way to wake up than this. His hand slides over my stomach and I pull him closer to me as his lips meet mine. He groans but then pulls away, making me pout. He chuckles and then says, "Come here, I have a surprise for you."

"A house and a graduation gift? You're too much!" I tease.

He laughs and when we turn into the living room, I see Ruth sitting on the sofa with a cup of coffee and a big box on the floor in front of her. It's not wrapped, it's not even taped. the folds of the box are open just slightly. I look at Jay in confusion, but he just smiles back. "Open it."

Hesitantly, I walk forward but then stop in my tracks when the box *moves.* My heart beats faster. I get down on my knees and grab the box with shaky hands but before I can open it, I hear the tiniest little whimper come from inside. My head shoots back to Jay.

"Stop," I say. "It's not." My voice immediately breaks. All he does is laugh.

Moving quickly now, I pull the box open and look inside. At the bottom is a perfect, fluffy, yellow puppy with black eyes and the sweetest black little nose. The tears are flowing like a river now and thanks to therapy, I embrace them.

"Jay," I croak as I pick the puppy up and hold it tightly to me.

Jay leans down next to me and pets the puppy as he kisses me on the cheek. "It's a girl," he says.

"A girl," I whisper.

I can't help but let my mind wander back to that little girl who always wanted a puppy. Who wanted someone to love and be loved back. The tears come faster as I realize these dreams are finally coming true. I feel her tongue on my cheek and she kisses me over and over and I squeeze her tight to me. "Oh sweet girl, you are going to be so happy with us!"

"What do you want to name her?" Jay asks.

"Hazel," I answer immediately as I put her down and let her little puppy feet run around the living room.

"Wow. That was fast." He chuckles.

"Hazelnut is my favorite flavor to add to coffee and I have always said to myself if I ever got a puppy, it'd be a girl and I'd name her Hazel."

"Hazel," he repeats before adding, "I love it."

Ruth is beaming down at us as she pets Hazel who is now her feet. Jay brings me in for an embrace and just as he does, Hazel leaps over to us and jumps in my arms, wanting to be a part of the family hug.

It isn't even nine a.m. on graduation day and it's

already the best day of my life.

We're at the ceremony now and I'm lining up with the other graduates. Jay kisses me goodbye as he and Ruth go find their seats and I find my correct spot in line. I recognize some faces around me from various classes I've taken, and I feel a quick twinge of jealousy when groups of them get together to take selfies, clearly close after years of getting to know one another. I never got that opportunity and right as I feel more resentment towards Loraine start to creep in, it disappears before I even have to push it down. The hold she has always had on me is slowly fading with each happy day that passes in this beautiful new life that I've found. I have people who love me, ready to cheer me on as I walk across the stage, and never in a million years did I think today would look like this.

It seems like it takes an eternity to get to the J's, but eventually it's my turn and I'm standing on the side of the stage waiting for my name to be called. The nerves and excitement coursing through my veins in anticipation.

"Emma Marie Johnson," the announcer calls and I carefully step on the stage, being careful not to trip in my heels. I look up in the stands and beam when I see Jay, Jessica, Ruth, and to my surprise even Robert, and they're all standing and cheering for me. I laugh to myself knowing Jessica probably found Jay solely based on the pictures I've shown her. It doesn't surprise me one bit that she would find and introduce herself to someone she doesn't know. She is so bold and I love her for that. And then I actually laugh out loud when I see her cover her mouth on one side with her hand and point to Robert who is sitting next to her with the other and mouth "Oh my GOD."

After the ceremony, the five of us go grab lunch at a popular local joint down the street. Jessica gets along with Jay great which makes me even happier. But it makes me ecstatic that she and Robert seem to be unable to stay away from one another. They have been in a constant conversation since we left graduation, their bodies close, but not touching, as if magnets.

Jay grabs his margarita and lifts it into the air. "To Emma!" he toasts.

"To Emma!" the rest of the table repeats.

I take a moment to look around the table at these people who have shown up today to celebrate me. My whole life I thought that a family had to look a certain way. A mom, dad, children, maybe even a dog. But that's not always the case. Family is who you make it. Family is people that love and support you. A family does not need to be blood. I've learned from experience that just because you're related to someone does not make them family. Not even close. I have a family now. It may not look as I thought, but it is better than I ever imagined.

# Epilogue

## Two Years Later...

A small handful of eyes land on me as the music erupts inside the venue. My shaky hands clench on to the stem of my bouquet as I start to make my way down the aisle. My eyes glue to Jay who is beaming at me, tears forming in his red eyes, he wipes one with his finger and the sight of it relaxes me. I let out a laugh that turns into a sob and smile back at him, unaware now of all the eyes on us. He is all I see.

There aren't many people here. We have only a total of about thirty guests at our wedding, but I wouldn't have it any other way. Jay's family, Jessica, some friends I have gotten close to at my job over the past couple years and some of Jay's coworkers as well who have turned into friends. It is intimate and perfect.

No one is walking me down the aisle, even though Ruth, Robert, and even Jessica offered. I laughed when Jessica suggested it and told her no way, her only duty is maid of honor. Besides, it felt right to walk myself down the aisle. I was my own caretaker, cheerleader, motivator, parent, and more for so many years. I feel almost proud of that as I make my way closer to Jay.

I glance at Jessica who is waiting in her maid of honor spot by the altar, Hazel's leash in her hand because yes, Hazel is a bridesmaid too. She smiles at me with a smile so big it's as if this were her own wedding. Tears stream down her face only adding more to my own. I use the handkerchief Ruth gave me while we were getting ready earlier to dab at my cheeks and under eyes.

Robert is next to Jay and when I look at him next, he has the most genuine smile on his face. He nods at me as if saying "you're so close, keep going." It's fitting that Jessica is my maid of honor and Robert is Jay's best man. They started dating about a year and a half ago and have been inseparable ever since. They've spent that time living in Robert's van together and traveling the country. Now they are planning to settle down in Austin and we are ecstatic to have them so close to us. Jessica doesn't know it yet, but Robert is proposing next week. They're meeting us in Greece to join the second half of our honeymoon and we have a whole plan for him to do it while we're there.

Finally, after what feels like an eternity, I make it to the end of the aisle and hand my flowers to Jessica so that Jay can take my hands in his. I'm impatient to get to the kissing part, but I try to soak it all in. We are starting a new chapter today. Not just as husband and wife though. Jay just doesn't know it yet. Those two pink lines from the test I took this morning flash back into my mind. I didn't want to tell Jay over the phone that we're having a baby, so I plan to tell him the minute we get a moment to ourselves. Our beautiful, perfect, happy little family is growing. I already know Jay will be the best dad in the whole world and I will finally get to be the mother I have always wanted to be.

"You look beautiful." Jay whispers to me and I beam at him as everything I've ever dreamt for comes true right before my eyes.

www.ingramcontent.com/pod-product-compliance
Lightning Source LLC
Chambersburg PA
CBHW030010070526
44668CB00015B/835